PROMISES

"I've been saying all along that those Martins are bad news." Jessica smacked the dashboard with her palm for emphasis.

"That's not exactly how I would put it, but I have to agree that Steven would be better off without Betsy around," Elizabeth said.

"And that's why we don't want Betsy to *be* around any longer than she has to," Jessica declared.

"Jessica Wakefield!" Elizabeth exclaimed. "Betsy's sister just died. Imagine what she must be going through right now. We have to be nice to her."

"All right, Liz," Jessica said after a few seconds' thought. "I'll try to be nice to Betsy Martin, OK?"

"OK," Elizabeth agreed.

At least for the moment, Jessica added to herself.

SWEET VALLEY HIGH

PROMISES

Written by
Kate William

Created by
FRANCINE PASCAL

BANTAM BOOKS
TORONTO · NEW YORK · LONDON · SYDNEY · AUCKLAND

RL 5, IL age 12 and up

PROMISES
A Bantam Book / January 1985

7 printings through January 1987

Sweet Valley High is a trademark of Francine Pascal

Conceived by Francine Pascal

Produced by Cloverdale Press Inc.

Cover art by James Mathewuse

ISBN 0-553-26765-5

Published simultaneously in the United States and Canada

*Bantam Books are published by Bantam Books, Inc. Its trademark, consisting of
the words "Bantam Books" and the portrayal of a rooster, is Registered in
U.S. Patent and Trademark Office and in other countries. Marca Registrada.
Bantam Books, Inc., 666 Fifth Avenue, New York, New York 10103.*

PRINTED IN THE UNITED STATES OF AMERICA

O   16   15   14   13   12   11   10   9   8

PROMISES

One

"Tricia, you can't leave us," Elizabeth Wakefield whispered, her large blue-green eyes filled with tears. Her heart ached as she looked down at the frail figure on the hospital bed.

No one had expected it to happen so soon. Or so suddenly. The doctors had said Tricia Martin was fighting a losing battle against leukemia, but she was so brave and full of life, Elizabeth had never fully believed there was no hope for her brother Steven's girlfriend. That is, not until Elizabeth had entered the room a few minutes earlier and found Steven slumped in a chair by Tricia's side.

Tricia's eyes were closed, and her face was paler than any Elizabeth had ever seen. The strawberry-blond cloud of hair that framed Tricia's delicate features was the only splash of

1

color against the stark white of the hospital linen.

"Oh, Tricia!" Elizabeth leaned down and gently took Tricia's hand, careful not to jostle any of the tubes that fed into her slender arms. Tricia's eyes fluttered open, then looked to Elizabeth's left. "Mr. and Mrs. Wakefield . . . and Jessica—" Slowly, and with great care, Tricia turned her head ever so slightly toward Elizabeth's identical twin sister, who stood near the door to Tricia's room. The corners of her mouth turned up in a gentle smile.

Jessica studied the floor intently, tracing the outlines of the linoleum tiles with the toe of her sandal. She had always made it clear that she disapproved of Tricia's family—her alcoholic father and wild, uncontrollable older sister, Betsy— and she'd used every devious scheme she could think of to get between Tricia and Steven. Yet here was Tricia, sweet and gracious to the very end. A single tear trickled down Jessica's cheek.

"Hey, no crying allowed!" Tricia's voice was barely louder than a whisper, but her tone was unusually forceful. "You've got to believe that these last few months have been the happiest of my life." She looked at Steven and held his gaze meaningfully. Her own tears threatened to break loose as she studied her dark-haired boyfriend, his handsome face lined with sorrow, his eyes ringed from lack of sleep. Quickly she shifted her attention back to Elizabeth, Jessica, and their parents.

"The happiest of my life," she repeated,

"because of you. I almost feel as if I'm part of the family."

As she pronounced the word "family" a dark expression flitted across Tricia's face. The look was gone as quickly as it had come, but Elizabeth didn't miss it. At first, she thought it was because it hurt Tricia to speak. Then she realized it was more than that. Most likely Tricia was thinking about her own family. Not even in Tricia's last hours could her father and sister be counted on to be with her. That was probably even more anguishing than the physical pain Tricia had been in.

Tricia gave a tiny, weak sigh. Clearly, even a few sentences of conversation drained her. Thoughts of her family couldn't help. Elizabeth could see that Tricia was fighting just to keep her eyes open. No wonder, Elizabeth thought, that her mother had phoned her and Jessica at Cara Walker's post-basketball-game victory celebration and told them to come to the hospital immediately. It looked as though Tricia couldn't hold on much longer.

Alice Wakefield took a step forward. "We love you, Tricia," she stated simply.

Ned Wakefield joined his wife at the foot of Tricia's bed. "We always said Steven knows how to pick the best," he said, trying hard to keep his voice light.

Tricia responded as best she could, summoning up her last reserve of strength to match his teasing tone. "Well, he must have learned from you, Mr. Wakefield."

Jessica watched the scene with growing amazement. How on earth did Tricia manage to be so heroic? Jessica's own day could easily be ruined by something as minor as a run in her stockings. But Tricia kept right on smiling in the face of death and showed the courage of a female Luke Skywalker. Jessica remembered what Elizabeth had told her not too long ago—that she should quit judging Tricia by her family and that no matter what people said about the other Martins, Tricia was noble from head to toe. *Well, maybe Elizabeth is right*, Jessica thought a little begrudgingly.

Now Tricia's gaze was back on Steven. "I guess I learned a little something about picking the best, too," she added softly. "I knew he was the one the very first time I saw him. . . ."

Alice and Ned Wakefield glanced at each other and then nodded to their daughters. It was time to say their final farewells and to give Steven and Tricia a few moments of privacy.

Elizabeth gave Tricia's hand a gentle squeeze. "Bye, Trish," she whispered, holding back a torrent of tears. As she walked away from the bed, the tears began to stream down her pretty face.

Jessica took several steps forward. "Tricia, I—I'm really sorry . . . I mean I—" For once she was at a loss for words.

"Jess, there's nothing to apologize for," Tricia said generously.

Jessica silently took back every nasty thing she had ever said about her brother's girlfriend.

"Well, take care," Jessica managed feebly. What could you possibly say to someone you knew you'd never see again?

The twins' father swallowed furiously against the lump in his throat as he leaned over and kissed Tricia goodbye. Alice Wakefield followed suit, also embracing her son before turning toward the door. The twins and their parents filed solemnly out of the hospital room.

"Remember, Steven?" Tricia asked, when his family left and the two were alone. "Remember that first time I saw you?"

Steven hoisted himself up and moved over to the edge of Tricia's bed. "I'll never forget," he told her, cupping his large hands around her pale face. "When I close my eyes, I can still see exactly the way you looked, splashing your feet in the ocean and trying to catch raindrops on your tongue. While everyone else on the beach ran as fast as they could to get out of the rain, I joined you at the water's edge. . . ."

"All those people missed the best part of the day," Tricia remembered joyfully, but her voice was painfully weak.

"You looked so beautiful that day." Steven bent down and kissed her forehead. "You still do." Suddenly his face wrinkled up, and he let out a choked sob. "Tricia, don't go," he cried. "Please stay with me." He dropped his head in his hands, his body racked with grief.

Tricia's fingers found Steven's body. With the final bit of energy left in her, she lifted her hand slightly and rested it on his knee. His sobs quieted.

"Steve, it's time," she said. "I can't keep going much longer. I want the pain to stop. Steve. You've got to let go now. Please. For me."

Steven lifted his head and wiped away his tears with the back of his hand. "For you, Trish. I'll do anything for you."

"Anything?"

"Whatever you want." Steven willed himself to smile for Tricia's sake.

"Well, there is something."

"Name it."

"My sister."

"What about Betsy?" To himself Steven added, *she couldn't even pull herself together enough to be here tonight.*

"Take care of her."

"Of Betsy?" Steven was incredulous.

"Steve, she has no one left to turn to. My father . . . well, when Mama died, just like this"—Tricia gestured feebly at the life-sustaining equipment—"he fell apart, drank himself into a stupor, then took off and didn't come back for months. I don't see why it'll be any different this time." She paused for a moment as if to regain her strength. Then she took a deep breath and continued. "And when he disappeared, that's when Betsy started getting into trouble. You know, she wasn't always like this." Tricia's eyes grew misty. "When we were kids, we were as close as two sisters could be. Just like Liz and Jess . . ." Her voice trailed off.

"I know, Trish. Be quiet now. You'll wear yourself out." Steven caressed Tricia's cheek with his fingertips.

"Say you'll do it, Steve. Look after Betsy."

"Tricia, I-I'm not sure anyone can look after her."

"Promise me," Tricia insisted.

Steven looked into her china-doll blue eyes. "I can't say no to you," he said softly. "I promise."

Tricia let out a small sigh. The conversation had clearly exhausted her. "I knew I could count on you. Steven, I love you."

"I love you, too, Trish."

"Steve, I'm so tired. I have to sleep, OK?" Tricia's voice was barely audible.

"Yes, it's OK," Steven murmured as Tricia closed her eyes for the last time.

Steven's face was streaked with tears as Elizabeth and Jessica shepherded him down the white corridors and toward the exit of the Joshua Fowler Memorial Hospital some time later. Close behind them, their parents followed in silence.

It's not possible, thought Elizabeth. *Tricia can't really be gone.* She put her arm around her brother's trembling body and guided him into the hospital lobby, her own tears flowing freely.

Suddenly Elizabeth gasped as a girl rushed through the hospital doors. She had the same slender build as Tricia, but a darker complexion and short brown hair that stuck out in disarray. Elizabeth froze in her tracks. The girl racing toward them was Betsy Martin!

"Tricia! Where's Tricia? I've got to see my sister!" Betsy's cries shattered the hush of the hospital lobby. Every eye in the large room was on her, and Steven took several strides in her direction. His jaw was set at a determined angle, his face grim.

Betsy rushed at him, weaving from side to side, her eyes bloodshot and wild, her arms flailing.

"My God, look at her," Jessica muttered contemptuously. "She couldn't walk a straight line if her life depended on it."

"I've got to see Trish!" Betsy screamed, oblivious to Jessica's cold stare.

A man in a starched white orderly's uniform hurried over to Betsy, a scowl on his face. "I must ask you to lower your voice, miss. Otherwise, you'll have to leave."

Betsy spun around on her heel, almost losing her balance. "Lower my voice?" she yelled. Even from several feet away, Elizabeth could smell the alcohol on Betsy's breath. Her heavy makeup was smeared under one eye, and her skimpy shirt was missing several buttons. "My sister's here. She's in this hospital. She's dying. Don't you understand?" Betsy shrieked. "Tricia's dying, and you're worried about me raising my voice!" She stumbled toward the orderly, her fists clenched tightly.

Steven stepped between them and drew Betsy to him. She pounded her fists against his broad chest. "Where's Tricia?" she screamed again. "Take me to Tricia!"

Steven stroked Betsy's head. "It's OK," he murmured. "You're going to be OK." Elizabeth could hear Betsy crying like a baby as she melted in Steven's arms. Steven steered her to the row of chairs at one side of the lobby, practically carrying her the last few yards.

"Did I say she couldn't walk a straight line?" Jessica asked. "She can't even walk. She's probably been in every bar in Southern California tonight."

"Stop it, Jess," Elizabeth pleaded. "Poor Betsy's going to need all the support she can get when Steven breaks the news." She looked over at her brother, who was holding Betsy's hands in his.

"Well, from what I've heard," Jessica said bitterly, "she should have the support of half the boys in Sweet Valley. Not to mention the ones from out of town."

"That's not the kind of support I'm talking about, and you know it," Elizabeth told her sister sternly. "Have some sympathy for her, will you?"

"Elizabeth is right," Alice Wakefield put in wearily. "Let's not have any squabbling tonight. It's been a hard enough evening without it."

Ned Wakefield put his arm around his wife's shoulder. "And it's not over yet," he added, watching as Steven spoke softly to Betsy.

Suddenly Betsy's cries pierced the air again. "No, Steven, no! It's not true! No-o-o. . . ." Her voice rose to a high, hysterical pitch. She rocked back and forth wildly.

Steven grabbed her and held her tightly until her screams dissolved into muffled sobs. Her head was buried against his shoulder, and she clung to him with all her might. Steven looked at his parents, helplessness written all over his face.

Ned and Alice Wakefield rushed to their son's side, Elizabeth and Jessica at their heels. Gently Mr. Wakefield loosened Betsy's grip on Steven and hugged her to his own powerful chest.

"I think what this young lady needs right now is a warm bed and a solid night's sleep." Ned Wakefield patted Betsy's back as she continued to weep quietly. "You, too, Steven. We're all going home."

"No!" Steven shot up from his chair. "Not Betsy. There's no one to take care of her at her house. We can't take her there." His face was a portrait of misery.

"I meant our home, Steven," his father explained gently. "Betsy's coming home with us."

For the first time since she'd come through the doors of the hospital, Betsy became silent. She looked up at the twins' father in astonishment.

Jessica, too, felt a wave of shock go through her. *Betsy Martin? In our house?*

Betsy seemed to echo Jessica's sentiments.

"Me?" she said softly. "You're going to take me home with you?"

"This instant," answered Ned Wakefield. "You and Steve will ride with me, and Alice will drive Steven's car back to the house. Girls." He addressed his daughters quietly. "Will you two be OK on your own in the Fiat?"

Elizabeth nodded.

"No, I couldn't go home with you—" Betsy began.

"Betsy, it's the best thing for you right now," Mrs. Wakefield insisted. "We just tried calling your father, and there was no answer. You shouldn't be all by yourself tonight."

Betsy shrugged out of Mr. Wakefield's grasp and turned toward his wife. "But I don't deserve it. Not after letting my sister spend her last night without so much as a goodbye from me." Her voice rose again, and she burst into another round of uncontrollable tears.

"Betsy, dear, there was nothing you could have done for Tricia that would have saved her," Mrs. Wakefield said gently.

"But I could have been there with her," Betsy sobbed. "Where I belonged. Instead—instead I was busy drinking and smoking everything I could get my hands on. . . ." Betsy's confession was punctuated noisily as she took in huge gulps of air.

"Oh, Tricia, forgive me—please." Betsy sank to her knees on the cold marble floor. "I promise —no, I swear—I swear I'll never touch any of that stuff again!"

11

Jessica eyed Betsy suspiciously. One of the worst girls in town resolving to turn over a new leaf? Jessica found it impossible to believe that Betsy Martin would ever be anything but bad news.

Two

"Betsy's resolution could be the one good thing that comes out of this evening," Elizabeth commented as she and Jessica made their way through the hospital parking lot to the little red convertible. She breathed in the cool night air, relieved to be away from the harsh white walls and the glaring fluorescent lights of Fowler Memorial.

"No way," Jessica replied. "She won't keep her promise. Just wait. Tomorrow Betsy will be right back to her old tricks. And staying under our roof, if her father doesn't turn up soon. God knows what everyone at school is going to say."

"Maybe everyone at school's going to say that Jessica Wakefield and her family are very special people for taking care of a poor thing like Betsy." Elizabeth unlocked the driver's door and slid into the car. Then she leaned over and opened the other door for her sister.

"Some poor thing," Jessica spat out as she settled into the passenger seat. "Honestly, Liz, I don't know how any sister of mine got so naive."

"I wouldn't call it naive. I prefer to think that I give people a fair chance."

"Right. If you met Jack the Ripper in a deserted alley, you'd probably think he was just out getting a breath of fresh air."

Elizabeth chose to ignore her twin's comment. She didn't have the energy to respond, not when her heart was swelled with sorrow over Tricia. She turned the key in the ignition and started the car.

"Hey, how come you always get to drive?" Jessica asked grumpily as Elizabeth pulled out, passing through the wrought-iron hospital gates. The twins could see the rear end of the Wakefields' rust-brown LTD up ahead of them.

"Jess, it's been a draining night for both of us. Do we have to get into this one again?" Elizabeth glanced at Jessica, who put on her best pout. "Look, you know Dad doesn't want you driving after all those tickets you ran up, especially the one you got on the way to Miller's Point."

Miller's Point, a scenic overlook, was well known as an after-dark hangout for couples from Sweet Valley High. Below it, the entire town of Sweet Valley was visible. But most of the couples there were too busy with other things to bother looking.

Jessica gave an exasperated sigh. "All because I was going a little faster than I should have been."

"A *little* faster? Come on, Jess. If I know you, you were probably driving like you were in the Indy Five Hundred."

"So, I paid for the ticket with the money I was saving up for a new stereo. Don't you think that's punishment enough?"

"Look, Jess. It's not my decision. Besides, you didn't need that new stereo. You know you're perfectly happy using mine." Elizabeth gave her twin a light swat on the arm.

"That's not the point," Jessica whined. She flipped on the radio and moved the dial from one station to another.

"Oh? What is the point?" asked Elizabeth.

"The point," answered Jessica, "is that I never should have gone up to Miller's Point that night in the first place. At least not with Paul Sherwood. He turned out to be the worst kisser in the entire galaxy. Sort of like a dead fish."

The two girls dissolved in giggles. After the evening's devastating events, it was a much needed release, and Elizabeth was grateful for the light moment. "Jess, you're too much," she said, laughing as she followed their parents' car down the twists and turns of the Valley Crest Highway.

"And speaking of Miller's Point," Jessica said, deftly moving the conversation back to the original subject, "did you hear who was there with Betsy Martin last week?"

"Jess, give her a break, won't you?" Elizabeth's light mood vanished instantly.

"Charlie Cashman *and* Jim Sturbridge, that's who. Both of them. At the same time. What do you think of that?"

"I think people can change, Jess."

"I swear, Liz, if we didn't look exactly alike, no one would ever guess that you were my very own twin sister."

It was true. Duplicate images on the outside, from their sun-kissed blond hair to their perfect, creamy complexions and their trim size-six figures, the girls were as different on the inside as two sixteen-year-olds could possibly be.

"How can you believe anything good about that girl?" Jessica continued. "Don't you remember the time she was racing around in Rick Andover's Camaro, high as a kite? When the police stopped them, they found more drugs in the glove compartment than you could find in a doctor's office!"

"I seem to recall a certain someone who was pretty keen on Rick Andover herself, once upon a time." Elizabeth flashed Jessica a pointed little grin.

Jessica played with the push buttons on the radio, switching from one song to another. "People do make mistakes sometimes," she said finally, defending herself.

"My point exactly," replied Elizabeth triumphantly as she turned the car onto Calico Drive.

16

"Betsy has made her mistakes, and now she's learning her lesson."

"Well, I just hope she learns it far away from me. It'll be a relief when drunk old Mr. Martin comes back and takes her off our hands. If he's on one of his binges, you don't think he'll stay out for more than a few days, do you?"

Elizabeth shook her head sadly. "I don't know what a man like Mr. Martin will or won't do. All I know is that he wasn't there when Tricia needed him, so why should he be there for Betsy?" Tears welled up in her blue-green eyes.

"I've been saying all along that those Martins are bad news." Jessica smacked the dashboard with her palm for emphasis. "It's about time Steven washed his hands of them forever."

"That's not exactly how I would put it, but I have to agree that Steven would be better off without Betsy around. I'm sure he won't go back to college until after the funeral services. And it's not going to help him get over Tricia to have her sister in the house."

"I knew sooner or later you'd see it my way." Jessica nodded smugly.

"Not so fast, Jess," Elizabeth warned. "I still say you have to be good to Betsy."

"Why? We don't want her to stick around any longer than she has to."

"Jessica Wakefield! Betsy's sister just died. Imagine what she must be going through right now. Think about it, Jess. How would you feel if you lost me?"

Jessica shuddered as she remembered a time

when she almost *had* lost her sister. Elizabeth had been in a terrible motorcycle accident because she, Jessica, was too busy having a good time to give Elizabeth a lift she'd promised her. Elizabeth had had to accept a ride on a motorcycle—a ride that had ended in disaster. Jessica's insides still froze when she pictured her sister lying in a coma, on the edge of death. It had been the worst time in Jessica's life. She prayed she'd never go through anything like that again.

"You win, Liz." The girls pulled into the driveway of the Wakefields' split-level house. "I promise to be nice to Betsy Martin, OK?"

"OK," Elizabeth agreed.

At least for the moment, Jessica added to herself.

Three

"Specialty of the house minipizzas again?" Elizabeth groaned as she and Enid Rollins pushed their lunch trays through the Sweet Valley High cafeteria line. "Honestly, they must make these things out of cardboard or something." She put a plate of pizza on her tray and helped herself to a container of juice and an apple. Then she looked around the crowded lunchroom for her boyfriend, Todd Wilkins.

There were people everywhere, poring over homework assignments, laughing with friends, table hopping, and spilling out onto the outdoor patio adjoining the cafeteria. *A day like any other day*, thought Elizabeth—for everyone else. Her own thoughts were never far from Tricia, and her concern about Betsy and her brother Steven colored every moment. Now, as she surveyed the noisy room, it was unnerving to see that while tragedy had struck in her life, the rest of the world hadn't just stopped.

"Liz, are you OK?" Enid put a reassuring arm around her best friend's shoulder, her big green eyes filled with concern.

"Yeah, I'll be fine. Thanks, Enid."

"I wish I could say something to make everything better, but getting over Tricia is going to take time. Right now all you can do is go about things as usual and just realize that your friends are behind you."

Elizabeth made an effort to smile. "Looks to me like you're in front of me," she joked lamely. Enid screwed up her face and gave Elizabeth a thumbs-down sign.

"I know—bad one." Elizabeth rolled her eyes. "But you're right, Enid. All I can do is try to enjoy this extra-special pizza as much as possible." The two friends giggled as they carried their lunch trays away from the food line.

"Do you see Todd anywhere? He called right after you did last night to offer his condolences." Elizabeth's voice became sad for a brief moment. "But anyway," she said, trying to push off the heavy mood, "when I saw him this morning, we decided we'd meet at lunchtime."

"Maybe he's outside," suggested Enid. They moved toward the patio just in time to see Todd and a number of others gathering around tall, lanky Winston Egbert. Winston was getting seated at one of the wooden picnic tables, the plate in front of him heaped with minipizzas.

"No way, Egbert," Bruce Patman was saying.

"You can't finish all four of those in less than four minutes."

"A night at the Beach Disco says he can," Todd challenged.

"You're on." Bruce nodded.

Enid and Elizabeth put their trays down at a nearby table and quickly joined the growing crowd to get a better view.

"Hey, good looking." Elizabeth circled her arm around her boyfriend's waist.

"Liz." Todd's voice was concerned. "How are you holding up?"

"Pretty well, all things considered. Enid's been cheering me up."

"Glad to hear it." The lean, handsome basketball player smiled down at Elizabeth. His coffee-brown eyes crinkled at the corners in a way that never failed to make her pulse speed up. Being next to Todd felt particularly special that day, because their awful near break-up was finally safely in the past. Todd gave Elizabeth an affectionate squeeze. "This ought to cheer you up even more." He gestured toward Winston, who, true to form, was going through an elaborate and hilarious pantomime of fastening his napkin around his neck to make a bib. "You're just in time to see me win us a night on the town." Todd pushed a lock of wavy brown hair out of his eyes.

"Well, I'm with Bruce, for once," put in Lila Fowler. "I think it's impossible."

"Lila, my sweet," clowned Winston, patting his stomach, "never underestimate the powers

21

of the Starch King. Ah, Elizabeth," he added, catching sight of her and making a little bow in her direction, "will you do the honors?" He pointed to the watch on her wrist.

"But, of course, Your Highness." Elizabeth looked at the second hand of her watch. "We'll start in about thirty seconds—at exactly ten after."

Winston took a swig of punch, then put the glass down noisily.

"OK, Win," Elizabeth said, studying her watch. "On your mark—get set—go!"

Winston took the first pizza and gulped it down in two huge bites. He stuffed the second one into his mouth and made exaggerated chewing motions.

"Trust Winston to turn this into a one-man comedy show," Lila muttered, tossing her long, wavy, light brown hair over one shoulder.

Winston followed the second pizza with a large swallow of the pink punch and started in on the third.

"Atta boy, Win," Elizabeth said. "Two and a half more minutes to go."

But Winston was slowing down. It took him four bites and a few dozen played-down chews to finish the third pizza.

"Looks like some lucky lady and I are going to the Beach Disco on you, Wilkins." Bruce Patman jostled Todd with his elbow.

Winston shot Bruce a look that clearly said, "If my mouth weren't stuffed full, I'd tell you where you're *really* going." But Bruce's jibe had spurred Winston on. Half the fourth pizza had already disappeared. Winston's goofy theatrics were replaced by a look of intense concentration.

"One more minute," Elizabeth called out. "You're going to make it."

"Keep on munching, Winston," shouted Enid.

"You can do it," added Roger Barrett, his arm around his girlfriend, Olivia Davidson.

"Twenty seconds," Elizabeth told Winston.

He popped the last bite into his mouth.

"Ten . . . nine . . . eight . . ."

Winston swallowed hard, took another swig of punch, and broke into a huge, ear-to-ear grin.

"Way to go, Winston!" yelled Todd. Then he slapped Bruce on the back. "This beautiful woman and I are all set for Friday night at the Beach Disco." He grabbed Elizabeth and spun her in the air.

Roger and football captain Ken Matthews hoisted Winston onto their shoulders and paraded him across the patio and onto the lawn, several others following.

"Make way for the Starch King," Enid shouted as they circled around one of the big oak trees on the Sweet Valley High campus. Olivia grabbed a couple of spoons from a lunch tray and clanged them together to herald Winston's triumph.

As the procession wound down, Regina Morrow came up beside Elizabeth and Todd, lunch in hand. "What's going on?" she asked.

"Hi, Regina. You just missed all the action." Elizabeth mouthed her words clearly so her deaf friend could read her lips. "I think Winston set a school record for pizza eating." She filled Regina in on Winston's feat. "And speaking of pizza," she added, as Enid approached, "we were just going to tackle ours. Why don't you join us?"

By the end of the lunch period, Elizabeth felt a lot more like her old self. Todd, Enid, and Regina kept her spirits up, cracking one silly joke after another about the pizza. In the end, no one finished more than half a pizza, deciding Winston had eaten enough for everybody.

Enid was right, Elizabeth thought. Her friends were behind her one hundred percent, and it really did help. But as the school day drew to a close, she couldn't avoid slipping into thoughts of Tricia. And more than once, she found herself worrying about Tricia's sister. Poor Betsy had no one to help her through her day, to joke with or talk to. *She must be so lonely, so frightened*, Elizabeth thought as she walked home from the bus stop after school. *If only Betsy had friends like mine. . . .* She kicked absently at a pebble. *Well, if there's one person she can count on, it's me*, Elizabeth decided. She stepped up her pace, determined to talk to Betsy as soon as she reached home.

As she pushed open the front door of the Wakefield house, Elizabeth was greeted by blaring music. "Hello? Who's home?" she called out. She knew Jessica was at cheerleading practice and her parents were still at work. "Steve? Betsy?" Elizabeth dropped her books on the marble coffee table and headed for the study, where Betsy had spent the night. Even with the door shut tight, the blast of the radio was almost deafening.

Elizabeth gave a tentative rap at the door. There was no answer. What could Betsy be doing in there with the music so loud? Elizabeth wondered. She was almost afraid to find out. She conjured up images of a smoke-filled room, half-empty bottles littering the red Oriental rug, Betsy sprawled on the sofa. Maybe she wasn't even alone. Maybe she had a boy in there.

No, Elizabeth told herself sternly. *You've got to give her the benefit of the doubt. After all, just last night you heard Betsy swear she was going to behave herself.* Elizabeth knocked a little harder. Nothing. Well, maybe Betsy couldn't hear her with the music turned up so loud. Hesitantly Elizabeth turned the doorknob and pushed the study door open just a crack.

Elizabeth's eyes widened with surprise. She had envisioned the worst, but she wasn't prepared for what she actually saw. Betsy was seated at the big mahogany desk, her back to the door—and she was hard at work! Elizabeth opened the door wider and stuck her head inside. Now she could see that Betsy, clad in a pair of cut-off jeans and a T-shirt, was leaning over a sketch pad, doing a pencil drawing. Elizabeth cleared her throat. "Betsy?" she said loudly.

Betsy whirled her head around, looking behind her like a frightened animal. "Oh, Elizabeth." Her shoulders relaxed. "Hi," she said flatly. Then she turned back to the desk and continued drawing. Elizabeth couldn't quite make out what she was working on.

"Betsy, I came to see if you wanted to have a brownie and a glass of milk with me," Elizabeth said above the music.

"A glass of milk—the good girl's drink," Betsy commented cynically. "I guess I'm going to have to get used to that."

"Should I take that to mean yes?" Elizabeth asked.

Betsy didn't look up from her drawing for a second. "Take it any way you want."

Elizabeth sighed. Getting through to Betsy wasn't going to be easy. Maybe she should quit while she was ahead. Perhaps all Betsy wanted was to be left alone. But just as she was about to walk away, Elizabeth remembered how supportive Enid had been at lunchtime. *Everyone needs that*, Elizabeth thought, *even Betsy Martin*. She drew a deep breath and resolved to try once more.

"I didn't know you were an artist, Betsy." Elizabeth took a small step into the study.

Betsy put down her pencil. "I like to draw," she said simply.

"That's great." Elizabeth's voice rang with enthusiasm. "How long have you been doing it?"

Betsy shifted around in her chair so she was

26

facing Elizabeth. Her expression softened. Elizabeth had the feeling that no one had ever taken an interest in Betsy's sketching before. "I guess ever since Mama died," Betsy answered. "I discovered that I could lose myself in it." She frowned slightly. "Sometimes it's the only thing that keeps me going."

As Betsy talked, Elizabeth went over to the radio. "Mind if I turn the volume down a little?" Betsy shook her head. "It doesn't bother you to have music so loud when you work?" Elizabeth questioned.

"I guess I'm used to it," Betsy explained. "At home, it blocks out the sound of Dad stumbling around and the neighbors fighting. . . ." Suddenly Betsy's face hardened again. "But you wouldn't understand those things."

Elizabeth seated herself on the sofa. "I certainly understand how you feel about your artwork. I think it's probably how I feel about my writing." Betsy seemed to be thinking over Elizabeth's words. "It's like having a friend who you know will always be there," Elizabeth continued. "When all else fails, I can always get some comfort or satisfaction from my writing."

Betsy's hard expression disappeared, and she nodded vigorously. Elizabeth sensed that she had hit home. "Yeah, I remember when I was at Sweet Valley High, you used to write for the school paper," Betsy said. "What was it called?"

"*The Oracle*. I'm still writing for it. In fact, I do the 'Eyes and Ears' column now." Elizabeth was referring to her weekly gossip column in the Sweet Valley High newspaper.

"Do you ever write for yourself? Like poems or stories or stuff?" Betsy pulled her chair out from behind the desk and drew nearer to the sofa.

Elizabeth hesitated. Her heart was set on being a famous author one day, and she already had drawers full of poetry and fiction she'd written over the years. But it was a secret ambition. Only a special handful of people knew how much her writing really meant to her. Ordinarily Elizabeth guarded this dream with silence.

But Elizabeth realized Betsy was starting to let down the wall she had built around herself. Certainly Betsy deserved to have Elizabeth open up to her in return. "Just between you and me," Elizabeth said slowly, "I do write for myself. All the time. But I'm kind of, well, shy about it. I don't talk about it much."

"I understand. It's a real private thing, isn't it?" Betsy leaned forward in her chair. "Not too many people know about my drawing either." She paused, and her face fell. "It's just as well. I've done such a great job of messing up everything else in my life, I feel like I'd better keep this part of me separate, or it'll get ruined, too." A note of bitterness crept into her voice.

"It can't be that bad," Elizabeth said gently.

Betsy looked down at the floor. "You don't have to try to make me feel better, Liz. I know what people say about me. About the booze, the pills, the guys. And it's all true."

28

Elizabeth put her hand on Betsy's knee. "Well, it doesn't have to be, Betsy. You just have to do more drawing and less of the other things, right?"

Betsy brightened a little. "Yeah. And I think my drawing's improving all the time."

Elizabeth smiled. "I'd sure like to see what you're working on now."

Betsy's face flushed. "I don't think so."

"Oh, come on, Betsy, please?"

"What if you don't like it?"

"Don't be silly."

"I don't know, Liz."

"Just a peek?" Elizabeth asked.

"Well—OK." The girls went over to the desk, and Betsy turned her sketch pad toward Elizabeth. On it was a portrait of Tricia. It was so skillfully rendered, with such grace and feeling in the lines, that it left Elizabeth speechless.

"I like to draw happy memories and people I love," said Betsy. "So what do you think?"

Elizabeth felt her eyes grow moist. "It's absolutely beautiful."

"Really?"

"Betsy, if your other drawings are even half as good, I'd say you're a tremendously talented artist. I can really feel Tricia's presence when I look at this picture." Both girls were quiet for a moment, their thoughts on Tricia.

Finally Elizabeth broke the silence. "Steven would love this picture," she said.

"Wow, I can't believe you just said that. I was thinking the same thing when I was doing

29

this drawing." Betsy took one last look at the picture before closing her sketch pad.

"Where is Steven, anyway?" asked Elizabeth, tactfully steering the conversation away from the painful subject of Tricia.

"He drove up to school to get his assignments for the week. Said he feels like he needs a few more days at home before he's ready to jump into things again. He'll be back by dinner time."

Elizabeth nodded. Then, impulsively, she leaned over and gave Betsy a hug. In the short time since she'd opened the study door, Elizabeth felt that an understanding had developed between them. Betsy returned the hug. "Liz, I know it might not have seemed like it at first, but I appreciate your coming in here and talking to me. Really."

"Any time, Betsy."

Betsy smiled, her hazel eyes lighting up. "And now, if the offer's still good, how about those brownies and milk?"

Four

Jessica stood in the middle of Elizabeth's room, a pile of clothes at her feet. She examined a pink cotton blouse, decided against it, and tossed it into the pile along with the other rejects.

"For goodness' sake, Jess, it's a funeral, not a cocktail party." Elizabeth frowned.

Jessica paid no attention to her twin. "Maybe your navy silk shirt," she said. "Nice but proper." She went over to Elizabeth's closet and plowed through the neatly hung clothes until she found what she was looking for. She held the shirt up in front of her. "What do you think?"

"Jessica, they're burying the girl Steven loved. How can you be so concerned about the way you look?" Elizabeth tried hard to keep her voice level.

Jessica darted a glance of annoyance in her

sister's direction. "Lizzie, dear, *someone* in this family has to look respectable. To make up for having you-know-who with us."

"Jessie, *dear*," Elizabeth copied her twin's tone exactly. "Didn't I hear you promise just the other evening to give Betsy a fair chance?" She pulled a dark gray crew-neck sweater over her head.

Jessica buttoned up the navy shirt and surveyed herself in the full-length mirror on the back of Elizabeth's door. "That was before last night."

"What happened last night?" Elizabeth zipped up her skirt and stepped into her shoes.

"Only what was to be expected." Jessica looked in Elizabeth's jewelry box and selected a pair of tiny gold hoop earrings.

"Jessica, what are you talking about? Would it be too much for you to put it in plain English?"

"I'm talking about what time Betsy got home last night. Or should I say this morning? I heard her come in. The sun was already up."

Elizabeth sank into her cream-colored canvas armchair. "Are you sure?"

"Sure, I'm sure."

"But, Jess." Elizabeth moaned, distress and disappointment spreading over her face. "What about her promise? She seemed so determined. . . ."

"Liz, what's a promise to a girl like that? She's done worse things in her life than go back on her word."

"But I just talked to her yesterday, and she

32

was so—I don't know—ready, eager to make a fresh start. It was like I was seeing a whole new side to her."

"Well, I don't know about that, but I do know what I heard. And I heard her come in just in time to be here when everyone else got up. But it's not my problem. After the services, we'll be rid of her for good." Jessica gave a little wave, as if to dismiss the subject. She went over to Elizabeth's closet again and selected a pair of gray heels.

"Hey, what about your own shoes?" Elizabeth asked. "The ones you just bought? What's wrong with those?"

"But, Liz, these go so perfectly with my skirt. Can't I wear them?"

"Jessica, you spent a month's allowance on your blue shoes."

"Oh, OK. If that's the way you're going to be . . ." Jessica disappeared through the bathroom that connected her room with her sister's.

But a moment later she was back. In her hand Jessica held one blue pump. "I can't find the other one," she wailed.

Elizabeth had to crack a smile. "Frankly, Jess, I don't know how you managed to find one shoe in that mess." Jessica's room was in its usual state of disarray, looking as if it had been hit by more hurricanes than the South Sea Islands.

Jessica continued to stand in front of Elizabeth, a pleading look on her face. "All right already." Elizabeth sighed. "Wear my shoes. We're going to miss breakfast if you take any longer."

33

Without hesitation, Jessica slipped into Elizabeth's gray shoes, and the corners of her mouth turned up. As usual, she'd gotten what she wanted.

Alice Wakefield was putting a basket of freshly baked muffins on the table as the twins entered the large, Spanish-tiled kitchen. Ned Wakefield was tending to the coffee and juice. Betsy, already at the table, sat silently, her head bowed.

"Morning, everyone," Elizabeth said softly. Betsy looked up, red-eyed. *From crying, or last night's partying?* Elizabeth wondered.

"Late night, Betsy?" Jessica slid into the chair next to her.

"Oh, did you hear me come in?" Betsy asked blankly. "I went over to the house to go through Tricia's things." Her face took on a faraway look. "I fell asleep on the sofa."

"Right," said Jessica in disbelief.

Elizabeth shot her sister an icy glare. Then she turned toward Betsy. "Are you all right this morning?"

Betsy nodded, but Elizabeth didn't miss the tear that trickled down one cheek. She took Betsy's hand and gave it a sympathetic squeeze.

Mr. and Mrs. Wakefield joined the solemn group at the table just as Steven came in. "Hi, everybody," he said quietly. His eyes were ringed and puffy, and he looked as if he hadn't slept a wink, but he made an obvious effort to keep his tone light. "Betsy, I brought you something I think you might enjoy." He put a large package in front of her before settling into his chair.

"For me?" Betsy seemed utterly bewildered. "But why?"

"Just open it," Steven coaxed. The whole family watched as she tore away the brown paper wrapping and took the lid off the white box.

"Oh, Steve!" Betsy exclaimed. "Wow, how terrific!" Inside the box was a complete set of acrylic paints and several brushes of different sizes.

"Liz told me that you like to sketch," Steven said, "and I thought maybe you'd want to try your hand at painting, too."

Betsy blushed furiously as she looked up at Steven. "It's the most perfect gift. . . . I don't know what to say."

"That's lovely, Steven." Alice Wakefield nodded in approval.

Betsy ran her fingers over the brightly labeled tubes of paint. Then she gazed at Steven again. "No one's ever brought me such a beautiful present. I mean, no one ever brings me presents at all." She paused, and then a dark veil of sorrow spread over her face. "No one, that is, except Tricia. . . ."

Lips trembling, Betsy lowered her head once more. Across from her, Steven stirred his coffee over and over, never lifting his eyes from the table. Elizabeth knew they were both lost in their memories.

The rest of the meal passed in silence.

"Ashes to ashes, dust to dust . . ." The minister pronounced the final words of the service as Tricia Martin's coffin was lowered into the ground.

Elizabeth shuddered against the damp morning fog and pulled her thin sweater tightly around her. She was solemn as she stood near the front of the shamefully small group of people who had come to pay their last respects to Tricia Martin. Some of the Sweet Valley High teachers were there, a handful of Tricia's classmates, and a few others. Betsy alone represented the Martin family. No other relatives had gathered for bittersweet reminiscences; no one had come to bestow one final declaration of love. Jim Martin, the girls' father, had not appeared. Though Betsy said nothing, her gaze had roamed over the crowd throughout the brief, simple service. The tiny ray of hope in her eyes had turned to sorrow-clouded disappointment and anger as she scanned the faces.

But now Betsy was still, one arm linked through Elizabeth's, the other through Steven's. Mr. and Mrs. Wakefield were at their son's side, their heads bowed. Even Jessica, standing next to her twin, wore a mournful expression as the first handful of dirt was thrown into the grave.

Suddenly Betsy gave a low, heart-wrenching moan, as if it were her very soul being buried in the earth. Her knees weakened, and Elizabeth felt her crumple to the ground.

"No! Dear God, no!" Betsy sobbed, beating the dew-soaked grass with her hands.

In a flash, Steven was kneeling down beside her. He wrapped his arms around her and rocked her back and forth. "It's OK," he crooned, forcing back his own tears. "Everything's going to be OK." He held Betsy tightly, stroking her head, until her grief-stricken wail gave way to subdued sobs and then to soft hiccups. Finally she was quiet.

Steven helped Betsy to her feet, continuing to hold her around the waist, as people filed past, murmuring their condolences.

"Such a sweet girl," whispered one of the women from the day-care center where Tricia had worked after school before she became ill. "Such a lovely girl."

"I'll miss her so much," a classmate of Tricia's told Steven and Betsy. The girl dabbed at her eyes with the edge of her sleeve as she walked away.

As the crowd dispersed, everyone offered a few words of commiseration. But even the most heartfelt and sincere expressions of sympathy couldn't do full justice to the memory of Tricia Martin. Warm, caring, generous Tricia. The girl who had once made Steven so happy. And the only real friend Betsy had ever had.

The last to offer his sympathy was Roger Collins, the handsome young faculty adviser to

The Oracle, Sweet Valley High's newspaper, and Jessica and Elizabeth's favorite English teacher.

"Tricia was one of my best students," he began. "She was a very special person. Betsy . . . Steven"—he gave each of them a long, hard hug—"I don't think anything I can say could possibly be enough." He shook hands with Ned and Alice Wakefield before turning to the twins. "Will you be in school this afternoon?" he asked quietly. Elizabeth and Jessica nodded. Then he was gone.

"I guess that's all," Elizabeth said in a small voice. It seemed to her that there should have been something more, some final outlet for the pain and sadness of Tricia's death. Instead, Elizabeth felt nothing but a dull, empty ache in the pit of her stomach.

Alice Wakefield put her arm around her daughter's shoulder. "Yes, it's over," she said. Then she turned to Steven and Betsy. "Are you kids going to be all right without us?"

"We'll be fine," Steven told her. "You and Dad go on to work. I'll drop Liz and Jessica off at school, and then . . ." His voice trailed off as he looked at Betsy.

"And then you and Betsy go back to our house," Ned Wakefield finished. "Betsy, you'll stay with us until . . . well . . . for the next few days." He glanced at his wife, who gave a quick nod.

Elizabeth could see Jessica stiffen. She also saw Betsy cast one last futile look around her for her father and then shake her head in resignation.

"Call if anything comes up," Alice Wakefield told Steven. "Your father will be in court, arguing a case, but I should be in my office all afternoon." The twins' father was one of Sweet Valley's most successful lawyers, and their mother worked as an interior designer.

Mrs. Wakefield embraced Betsy. "We know how hard this must be for you," she said, "and we're here for you if you need us."

Betsy nodded but remained silent. She didn't utter a sound until after the elder Wakefields had left and she was seated in the front passenger seat of the little yellow VW. As Steven turned the key in the ignition, Betsy put her hand on his arm. "You're taking me to Kelly's," she said, not a drop of emotion in her voice.

In the backseat, Elizabeth's mouth dropped open in startled dismay. Kelly's, the seediest, most disreputable bar in Sweet Valley, was bad enough on a Saturday night, but before lunch in the middle of the week? Only the most hardcore, bottom-of-the-barrel drinkers were in there now.

Jessica leaned over and nudged Elizabeth in the ribs with her elbow. "See? What did I tell you?" she hissed in her sister's ear. "The old Betsy's back. And not more than five minutes after Tricia's been put in the ground."

Steven turned toward Betsy. "I don't think I heard you right," he said firmly.

"Oh, I think you heard me fine," she said

flatly. "But maybe Mr. Picture Perfect Steven Wakefield doesn't know how to get to Kelly's." Betsy's voice took on a harsh edge. "Well, I could get you there blindfolded. Take the second right and drive straight out toward the beach—"

"I know where it is," Steven said patiently. "But that's not where we're headed." He steered the car in the other direction. "First we're taking Liz and Jess to school. And then we're going straight home."

"Home?" Betsy asked sarcastically. "What's that? And who are you to tell me where I can or can't go?" Her voice was rising.

"Betsy, don't get so hyped up," Jessica said coldly from the rear of the car. "I'm sure if Steve won't take you to Kelly's, you'll find some other guy who will."

Steven shot his sister a venomous look. Then he turned his attention back to Betsy. "I seem to remember a promise you made to yourself the other night. What happened?"

"Damn my promise!" Betsy shouted. "Why behave? Where's it going to get me, anyway? I mean, what's the use of trying to be like Tricia? She was the best person in the whole world, and look at what good it did her. . . ."

In the rearview mirror, Elizabeth saw Steven wince at Betsy's words.

"Betsy," he said, his voice thick with pain, "I know how much you're hurting right now. But Kelly's isn't going to help. It's not going to bring Tricia back to us."

Betsy was quiet for a while, obviously sharing Steven's anguish. When she spoke again, she was calmer. "Steve, I didn't mean to make you feel worse. It's just that I have nowhere else to go." She gave a forlorn sigh before continuing. "Oh, I heard your parents. But how long can that last? Till my Dad comes to get me? We both know that's what your father was going to say before. Well, what if he never comes? Then what?" Betsy buried her face in her hands.

As Steven drove he could hear Tricia's last words echo in his head as clearly as if she'd been sitting right next to him: *Take care of her, Steve. She has no one left to turn to.*

"Betsy," he finally said, his voice leaving no room for argument. "Kelly's is out. You're coming home with me."

He pulled up near the white-columned entrance to Sweet Valley High. "From now on," he announced, to the utter shock of both Elizabeth and Jessica, "the Wakefield home is your home. For good."

Five

"OK, Jess, out with it." Cara Walker gave her best friend a little poke on the shoulder.

"Out with what, Cara?" Jessica asked, leaning on her elbow with studied innocence.

"Oh, come on, Jessica. You've been sitting there, staring into space, for the past half-hour. You've barely touched your lunch."

"Maybe I don't like what they're serving," Jessica replied.

Cara exchanged glances with Lila Fowler, across the school cafeteria table. The two girls rolled their eyes in exasperation.

"Look, Jess, I know week-old ham-and-cheese isn't your favorite, but somehow I don't think that's it," Cara said. "And I don't think it's the great trauma of Tricia's funeral, either. Oh, I'm sure you put on a good show this morning, but we all know she wasn't the most important person in your life."

"Yeah, Jessica," Lila put in, "what gives?"

Jessica threw up her hands. "Listen, can't a person have any privacy with you two around?"

"Privacy?" Cara tossed out. "What's that? I remember you once told me there were no secrets between friends like us. Of course, you were the one digging for information, then."

"And anyway," Lila added, "you know we're going to find out sooner or later. So you might as well tell us right now."

Jessica pushed the food around on her plate. "Well . . . I do need to talk to someone about it," she hedged.

Cara and Lila leaned forward, ready to devour Jessica's every word.

"But you've got to promise not to spread it around. I don't want anyone associating me with that girl."

"What girl?" Cara's brown eyes lit up in anticipation of a ripe piece of gossip.

"Oh, it's so horrible," Jessica wailed, raising her hand to her head dramatically. "It's Betsy Martin."

"That tramp?" Cara asked in disgust. "What's she up to this time?"

"That tramp," Jessica moaned, "has moved into my house!"

"No!" exclaimed Lila. "How positively awful—having to share your home with such low-class trash. Why, our stable boy has more class than Betsy Martin."

Lila's family was one of the wealthiest in Sweet Valley, and Lila never lost an opportunity to remind people that she was part of the upper class.

"It *is* awful," Cara agreed. "What happened, Jess? I thought she was supposed to leave after the funeral."

"That's what I thought. I mean, her father sort of disappeared when the hospital phoned him and told him Tricia was on the way out. You know—he went off to drown his sorrows or something," Jessica said. "But I just assumed he'd turn up for the funeral and Betsy would go home with him. I don't know why I thought I could count on someone like Mr. Martin." She glanced around the large cafeteria to make sure no one else was listening to their conversation. As she did, she noticed Winston Egbert walking by, his tray piled high with ham-and-cheese sandwiches. "Oh, no," she muttered. "What on earth is he going to do with all of those?"

"Haven't you heard?" asked Cara. "Winston wants to break the world pizza-eating record—seven extra-large pizzas in one sitting. He's practicing with those sandwiches. He told me he'll do anything to increase his capacity for starch."

The girls watched the tall, skinny boy settle down at an empty seat and begin to stuff sandwiches into his mouth. Several kids cheered him on.

"That boy will do anything for *attention*, you mean," Lila said, shaking her head.

"Where do you think he puts it all?" Cara

asked incredulously as the sandwiches rapidly disappeared.

"That's *his* problem," Jessica told her friends. "I've got bigger problems on my hands right now. Like Betsy. What am I going to do?"

"It *is* unfortunate," Lila said. "But there's got to be a solution." She twisted a strand of hair around her finger. "Can't you get your parents to ask her to leave?"

Jessica shook her head. "Everyone feels so sorry for her. It's 'Poor Betsy, no one to take care of her,' 'Poor Betsy, she's had it so rough.' But what about poor *me*?" Jessica stuck her lower lip out in a well-practiced pout. "Can you imagine what people are going to think when they find out who's practically become my second sister?"

Lila snapped her fingers. "I've got it!"

"What?" Jessica and Cara chorused in unison.

"It's so simple." Lila grinned smugly. "Look, you don't really believe Betsy's cleaned up her act, do you?"

"No way," replied Jessica. "Just this morning she was almost down on her knees, begging Steven to take her to Kelly's."

"Well, then, all you have to do," explained Lila, "is to go through her things sometime when she's not home. Find the goods. You know, pills, pot—whatever."

"Oh, Lila, that's perfect!" Cara gushed.

"Naturally, dah-ling," Lila drawled.

Jessica's blue-green eyes began to glow. "Right," she said. "And then I'll happen to oh-so-casually mention to my mother that I was looking for a pad of writing paper in the den and I found something that really worried me. I'll let her draw the rest out of me, of course.''

"Of course," agreed Lila.

"I wouldn't want to seem eager to tell on Betsy or anything. But it'll come out. And that'll be it for her. There's no way Mom will tolerate that kind of thing under our roof," Jessica finished triumphantly.

But before she had time to pat herself on the back, Olivia Davidson rushed over, a worried look on her face. "Have any of you seen Roger?" the frizzy-haired arts editor of *The Oracle* asked urgently. The three friends shook their heads.

As Olivia rushed off, Lila mimicked her. " 'Have you seen Roger?' Now why would I keep track of Roger Barrett? He's just another case of low-class trash in my book.''

"Seems more like a case of sour grapes to me, Lila," Jessica snickered. Lila had once tried to ensnare Roger, but she'd lost out to Olivia. She'd never forgiven either of them.

"Yeah, Roger might be poor," added Cara, "but he's definitely not low class. I'll bet he's going to set an Olympic track record one day—if he's not too busy finding a cure for cancer, or some other brilliant thing.''

"Think what you like," Lila said defensively. "But I couldn't care less about Roger Barrett. Or Olivia either, for that matter.''

Suddenly a cry of anguish filled the lunchroom. "Well, speak of the devil himself," observed Lila. "Looks like Liv found what she was after."

At the far end of the cafeteria, Olivia had her arms around her boyfriend, who was shaking his head back and forth in agony. A small crowd began to gather around them.

"Don't you think we should find out what's going on?" Cara was out of her seat without waiting for an answer. She rushed over to the other side of the room, Jessica following close behind. Lila remained seated.

Jessica spotted Elizabeth and Todd in the group of people who had gathered around Roger and Olivia. "Liz," she said, tugging at her sister's sweater. "What's happening?"

Elizabeth whirled around, a look of distress on her face. "It's Roger's mother," she answered. "She's had a heart attack! They don't know if she's going to make it!"

Cautiously Jessica turned the doorknob to the study. She pushed the door open just a crack and peered into the room. Empty. Betsy was nowhere in sight. So far, so good. Elizabeth was working late at the *Oracle* office, and no one else was home yet either.

Jessica opened the door farther and strode purposefully into the study.

One of Betsy's blouses was draped over the back of the lounge chair, and her comb and brush lay neatly on the little glass table. On the walls she had hung several of her sketches. In the corner of the room was her blue suitcase, open to reveal two stacks of neatly folded shirts and pants. Betsy's tennis shoes, a pair of brown boots, and some open-toed flats were arranged to one side. *God, it looks positively homey in here*, Jessica thought. *If I get rid of her now, it won't be a minute too soon.* She went straight to the suitcase and began digging around, careful not to misplace or disturb a single thing. Under the clothes was a small, red, zippered pouch. *This is it*, Jessica told herself triumphantly. *This must be where she keeps everything.* She zipped the pouch open, dumping out its contents: a lipstick, a tube of mascara, a thin enamel bracelet. Finally, everything was on the floor. *Darn!* Not a suspicious item to be found. Jessica shook her head in annoyance and put everything back into the red pouch. She continued to feel around in the suitcase, searching every side pocket and corner.

Suddenly her fingers touched something—a tiny rectangular box. A pillbox! Eagerly Jessica closed her hand around it and lifted it from the suitcase. It was a gold case topped with tiny mother-of-pearl chips. As Jessica unlatched it, a sly smile spread over her face. Pay dirt! The box was crammed with little white tablets. Jessica picked one up and turned it over in her palm. Some letters etched into the pills caught her eye. She took a closer look: B-A-Y-E-R. *Damn it!* They were nothing but plain old aspirin!

Jessica let out a shriek of frustration. She put the pillbox back where she'd found it and began opening drawers and closets. Frantically she sifted through everything in the study and came up with a big zero.

Exhausted, she sank down on the couch and gave a defeated sigh. Had Betsy really and truly decided to straighten out? Or was there some hiding place that Jessica had overlooked? She glanced around the study. No, she'd hunted everywhere. Her gaze finally came to rest on one of Betsy's drawings hanging on the wall across from where she sat. Jessica took a good look at it for the first time. It was a picture of three children playing tag in someone's front yard. *Not bad*, Jessica allowed. She turned her attention to the other sketches—equally well done. *Amazing*, she said to herself, *trashy old Betsy Martin's actually an OK artist. Even more than OK*, Jessica grudgingly admitted.

Betsy's sketch pad lay on the mahogany desk. Her curiosity now thoroughly aroused, Jessica went over and started flipping through it. There was a picture of some woman Jessica didn't recognize but who looked vaguely familiar; a series of nature scenes, including one beautiful sketch of the brook behind the Sweet Valley elementary school; and several drawings of Tricia. As Jessica studied the last of these, she felt a tiny pang of guilt. This had to be Betsy's most private and treasured possession. But Jessica brushed away the twinge of conscience and hurriedly turned the page. A jolt of shock shot through her body as she looked at the next picture.

49

"Oh, my God," she whispered to herself. The sketch pad slipped from her fingers and clattered onto the desktop.

Later that afternoon, Elizabeth stepped into her lavender sweater dress and fastened the row of tiny buttons that ran up the back. As she was choosing a pair of shoes to wear, the door to the bathroom that connected her room to Jessica's burst open.

"Liz, I've got to talk to you about Betsy," Jessica said as she plopped down on Elizabeth's bed. "It's urgent."

"Again, Jess? Todd and I are meeting Nicholas and Regina for dinner at the Box Tree Café. I don't want to be late." Elizabeth peered in the mirror as she pulled a brush through her spun-gold hair.

"Oh, Nicholas," Jessica sniffed. "I don't know why you bother with a bore like him."

Nicholas Morrow was Regina's handsome eighteen-year-old brother and one of the nicest guys Elizabeth had ever met. But he had recently committed the monumental sin of turning Jessica down when she'd made her interest in him clear. For that, he'd won a spot on her list of least favorite boys.

"Jessica, I probably shouldn't even grace that remark with an answer," Elizabeth told her twin, "but I seem to remember that not too long ago, Nicholas Morrow was the only thing on your mind."

Jessica shrugged. "Well, I've got much more important things on my mind now."

Elizabeth sighed. As usual, it was useless to argue with Jessica. "OK, Jess. Like what?" Elizabeth asked.

"Like Betsy Martin. She's got to go. You know, I can't even invite people over after school for a swim anymore. Not with that tramp lying around by our pool like she owns the place."

"Is that right, Jessica? Well, it just so happens that Enid was over for a swim the other day, and the three of us had a great time." Elizabeth slipped into a pair of low-heeled blue pumps. "I don't see why your friends should feel any differently."

"Oh, Enid." Jessica sniffed. "She's just another Betsy turned Goody Two-Shoes."

Jessica was referring to the fact that Enid had once hung around with a bad crowd of kids who were constantly in trouble with the law. But that part of Enid's life was over, and she'd never once been tempted to return to it.

"For your information, Jessica, Enid Rollins is one of the most generous, wonderful people in the world." Elizabeth stood up for her best friend. "But you didn't come in here to discuss Enid. You came to talk about Betsy, right?"

"Right. Betsy. Betsy and our brother."

"Our brother? How does Steven figure into this?" Elizabeth questioned.

Jessica jumped up and began pacing the room. "Oh, Liz, it's so awful," she wailed. "You wouldn't believe what I discovered in Betsy's room."

Elizabeth took Jessica by the shoulders. "And just what, may I ask, were you doing snooping around in her room?"

Jessica wiggled out of her sister's grasp and started examining her hands with intense concentration. She hadn't counted on having to explain her presence in the study to Elizabeth. She changed the subject abruptly. "What do you think of this new shade of nail polish I got? Too orange?"

"You don't really think you're going to get off that easily, do you, little sister?" Elizabeth was only four minutes older than her twin, but it sometimes seemed to her that it was more like four years. She fixed Jessica with a hard stare.

"Elizabeth, I hate it when you look at me that way." Jessica groaned. "If you absolutely must know the truth," she said, crossing her fingers behind her back, "I wanted to see those sketches you and Steven kept raving about. I mean, who would believe that Miss Tramp-of-the-Year is really a budding Leonardo da Vinci!"

Elizabeth frowned, thinking about how she'd feel if she found out that someone had gone through her writing. It was for this reason that she kept her work locked in her desk drawer. "You know you had no business poking around in Betsy's things. And I don't understand what this could possibly have to do with Steven, anyway."

"Liz, you saw her pictures, right?" Jessica asked. Elizabeth nodded. "Wouldn't you say she really cares about the things she draws? You know—all those pictures of Tricia, and that one of the cat and her kittens. And did you see the one of that woman? I'll bet you anything it's Betsy's mother. She looked sort of like her and Tricia," Jessica continued.

Again Elizabeth nodded slowly. "Betsy told me as much herself. She draws people and things she loves. But, Jess, I don't get what you're driving at." A note of annoyance crept into Elizabeth's voice. "Honestly, I don't know why you get such a kick out of these verbal cat-and-mouse games. When you came in here, you said you had something urgent to tell me. Why don't you just say it?" Elizabeth pinned her shoulder-length blond hair back with a navy-blue comb. "I don't want to make Todd wait."

"Well, big sister," Jessica began, "there was one picture she probably didn't show you. It was drawn with all the love and care of those other pictures." Jessica paused dramatically. "And it was of our brother!"

Six

Jessica slammed her locker shut. "Strike one," she told Cara Walker.

Cara shook her head sympathetically, her dark hair swinging from side to side. "Lila's plan backfired?" she asked.

"You said it," Jessica confirmed, her voice filled with irritation. "You know, I wouldn't be surprised if Lila purposely cooked up a scheme she knew wouldn't work, just so she could gloat about me getting stuck with Betsy. 'Oh, I couldn't imagine having to live in a charity home for that kind of riffraff,' " Jessica mimicked, tossing her head in a perfect imitation of Lila Fowler.

Cara giggled. "Only Lila could have put it better, dah-ling," she parroted. The girls walked down the hall to Cara's locker.

"So you didn't find anything?" Cara twirled her combination lock.

"Nope. And Liz was saying the other day that Betsy's been clean as a whistle ever since Tricia died. But she can't last. Not a girl like that." Jessica scowled. "And when she starts getting in trouble again, she's going to bring the whole Wakefield family down with her."

Cara stashed her books in her locker, and she and Jessica walked down the corridor to the cafeteria. "Cara," Jessica said in a low voice, "do you remember the time Betsy got hauled down to the police station for shoplifting, and Tricia had to leave school to go bail her out?"

"Do I remember? Who do you think told you about it?" Cara asked. "I had study hall with Tricia then. Boy, was that something. This monitor came in with a note for her, and—"

"I know the story," Jessica interrupted. "But what if something like that happens again? Who's Betsy going to turn to? Can you imagine *me* getting a folded-up note in class one day?"

Cara stopped by the water fountain and took a long, slow drink. She wiped her mouth with the back of her hand. "Actually, Jess, I don't think *you've* got that much to get nervous about. If you ask me, it's Steven you should be worrying over."

Jessica flinched. How did Cara know about Betsy's feelings for Steven? She'd made a point of keeping quiet on the subject. It was bad enough that Steven had gone out with one Martin, but the possibility of a second—especially when it was Betsy—was too horrible to think about. And certainly nothing to talk about.

Jessica took a drink of water. Then she turned back toward her friend. "Well, actually, Cara, I *didn't* ask you about Steven. But as long as you're volunteering your opinion, what makes you think I should be worrying about him?"

"Gosh, Jess. You don't have to get so huffy all of a sudden. It's just that people are starting to talk about Betsy and your brother being together all the time. Like in gym class, Caroline Pearce said she saw them at the Valley Cinema last night.

Jessica pounded her hand against a row of lockers they were passing. *Damn Caroline Pearce!* she thought. *Always acting so prim and proper, but she's got a tongue like a poisonous snake's.*

"Cara, *you* know how Caroline can take a perfectly innocent thing and twist it around so it comes out racier than a Bo Derek movie."

Cara opened her brown eyes wide. "Perfectly innocent? The way Caroline tells it, Betsy was all over him."

"For goodness' sake, what did I just say about the way Caroline tells it? Betsy probably just let Steve hold the door for her or something. Besides, you, of all people, should understand why Betsy might be a little interested in my brother."

For the longest time Cara had been crazy about Steven Wakefield. At one point, when Tricia Martin had been avoiding Steven, Jessica arranged for him to go out with Cara. But Steven's thoughts were never far from Tricia, and his relationship with Cara ended almost before it started. Steven discovered that Tricia had leukemia and was trying to make him forget about her to spare him the pain of losing her. Steven rushed to Tricia's side and never gave Cara another thought. Cara, on the other hand, still had her eye on Jessica's handsome brother.

Cara ignored her friend's obvious reference to her crush on Steven. It was Betsy's feelings she was discussing, not her own. "From what I've heard, Jess, Betsy's more than just a *little* interested in him. In fact, it sounds as if she's head over heels in love. And, Jessica, it's not just Caroline who's talking. It's all over town. They've been at the mall together; they've been to the beach."

"OK. So maybe Betsy likes him. Who wouldn't? He's handsome and smart and—"

"Jess, you don't have to convince me. But why would Steven spend so much time with Betsy unless he felt something for her?" Cara pushed open the swinging metal door that led to the cafeteria.

The girls got at the end of the lunch line, each taking a plastic tray, silverware, a glass, and a napkin. "Steven's only trying to be nice to Betsy." Jessica inspected a dish of mushy-looking fruit salad, made a face, and put it back on the cafeteria counter. "He's a good guy, and he knows how miserable Betsy must feel about her sister. That's all there is to it." Jessica's tone clearly indicated that the conversation was over.

"OK, if you say so, Jess."

"I do, Cara," Jessica stated emphatically. But she was beginning to waver. True, Steven didn't act as if he were in love. He didn't return Betsy's tender glances. At most, he offered a friendly smile. He hadn't reacted at all when their hands had accidentally touched as he reached for the cereal at breakfast. And, most importantly, he was still mourning for Tricia. Just that morning, Jessica had caught him staring at a photo he had of Tricia, tears glistening in the corners of his eyes.

But it was also true that he and Betsy were together almost constantly. Nice was nice, but Steven seemed to be going overboard. What reason, Jessica wondered, could he possibly have for lavishing so much attention on Betsy? If it wasn't love, what was it?

Jessica was still asking herself the same question when she got home from cheerleading practice that afternoon. She dropped her books on the living-room table, kicked off her tennis shoes, and headed toward the kitchen to get something cold to drink. As she passed the study, Betsy's voice floated out to the hall.

"No. I'm not stepping foot in that place again. My days at the Shady Lady are over."

Jessica stopped in her tracks. The Shady Lady was one of the sleaziest bars in town.

"Not Kelly's, either," Jessica heard Betsy add. "No, I'm not kidding."

Jessica moved closer to the study door, not

wanting to miss a word of Betsy's telephone conversation.

"I don't want to, not even for a few beers." Betsy was insistent. "Crunch, forget it."

Aha! thought Jessica. *So that's who Betsy's talking to.* Jerry McAllister had earned the nickname "Crunch" as the starting tackle for Sweet Valley High. When a knee injury had put Crunch off the football team for good, he'd dropped out of school, but his team nickname had stuck.

Now Crunch McAllister could usually be found hanging out in rundown bars, drinking himself into a stupor. It was Crunch who had caused Elizabeth's near-fatal accident. Drunk out of his mind, he'd lost control of his van and plowed into the motorcycle she was on. And now Crunch McAllister had had the nerve to call the Wakefield house! Jessica felt her blood boil.

"Listen, Crunch," Betsy was saying, "I'm starting to have a little respect for myself for the first time since who knows when." There was a pause. "I don't care *what* you think." Betsy's voice grew sharp. "*I* think I've got a good thing going, and I don't want to mess it up."

Jessica shuddered. "Good thing going"? Did that mean Steven?

"And, Crunch, I don't want you to mess it up, either. Don't you ever call me here again." Jessica heard Betsy slam down the receiver. Quickly she moved away from the study door and into the kitchen.

A few minutes later, as Jessica was finishing a glass of apple juice, Betsy wandered into the kitchen. "Hi, Jessica," she said. "I didn't know anyone was home."

"Hi, Betsy. Who was that on the phone just now?" Jessica's voice was sugary sweet and innocent.

"Oh, no one who matters," answered Betsy. "No one who matters at all."

"And is there someone who *does* matter?" Jessica prodded.

Betsy turned red. "Maybe," she replied frankly, running her fingers through her short, dark curls. "I mean, I hope so."

"Anyone I know?"

Betsy lowered her eyes. "It's—it's too soon to say anything," she stammered.

"I see," Jessica said slowly. There was no question about it. Betsy was in love with her brother. And all Jessica could do was hope against hope that he didn't return the feeling.

Seven

"I'm gonna love you forever," crooned Dana Larson, lead singer for The Droids, Sweet Valley High's favorite student band. "Love you forever and a day." Dana's rich alto voice filled the Beach Disco as Elizabeth and Todd made their way inside. The dance floor was already packed, couples swaying to The Droids' latest romantic tune. As the song wound down, Emily Mayer let out a ferocious drum roll, and Dan Scott, the bass guitarist, picked up the beat as the group went into a fast number. The lights flashed, and the crowd went wild.

"Big night," Todd said. "Looks like every person from here to Seattle is on that dance floor." He wound his arms around Elizabeth and drew her toward him. "And I'm with the most beautiful girl in the whole place," he whispered in her ear.

Elizabeth melted against Todd's broad chest and smiled up at him. It felt so wonderful to be with him like this and to have ironed out the problems they had recently had. It was the first time since even before the nightmarish evening of Tricia's death that Elizabeth had really been able to relax. She touched Todd's cheek with her fingertips and looked into his warm brown eyes. Tenderly he lowered his lips to hers and ran his fingers through her sun-streaked hair.

"Well, well, what do we have here?" Elizabeth was startled by a deep voice. She whipped around to see Bruce Patman, arms folded, a smirk on his face.

"Hello, lovebirds," he sneered. "I came to pay your way in tonight." He turned to Todd. "After all, a bet's a bet. But maybe the two of you would like to go somewhere a little more private."

"And miss all the action?" Elizabeth laughed. "Forget it, Bruce."

"Yeah, Patman," said Todd. "Cough up the loot. You can spare it."

Bruce pulled a thick stack of crisp green bills out of his wallet and peeled a few dollars off the top. "A Patman always makes good on his deals," he pronounced. "But how about we go double or nothing on Winston's next attempt?"

Todd shook his head. "I think I'll pass, Bruce. I don't want to push my luck."

"Suit yourself." Bruce shrugged. "And now, if you'll excuse me, I have a bit of romancing to do myself." He took off after a tall, statuesque brunette.

"Poor girl," Elizabeth commented.

"Oh, I wouldn't necessarily feel sorry for her. Some people go for arrogance. And anyway, Bruce *is* handsome."

"Not to mention fabulously wealthy."

"How could anyone forget that?" Todd and Elizabeth watched as Bruce led the girl onto the dance floor. "As a matter of fact, she doesn't seem to mind one bit," Todd noted. "And Bruce seems to have the right idea for once. Shall we join them in a dance?"

"Sounds good to me," Elizabeth agreed. She took Todd's hand, and they snaked their way through the crowd to the center of the floor, where Enid Rollins was dancing with her boyfriend, George Warren, a student at Sweet Valley College.

"Liz, Todd—hi! We were wondering when the two of you would get here." Enid flashed a big, warm smile.

"Yeah, we didn't want you to miss one minute of The Droids," George put in. "They're more terrific than ever tonight."

"They do sound hot," agreed Todd, as the guitarist, Max Dellon did a brief solo.

Todd spun Elizabeth around in the air, putting her down with a flourish. They made a perfect team as they danced under the flashing strobe lights, Elizabeth's smooth, graceful movements complementing Todd's more playful style.

Several songs later, they were still whirling

around the dance floor, grinning from ear to ear. Todd pushed a moist lock of wavy brown hair out of his eyes. "Whew! It feels great, but I could do with a cold drink," he said. "How about you, Liz?"

"A root beer would be great," Elizabeth replied. "See you later," she called to Enid and George, who were still going strong on the dance floor. She and Todd made their way through the packed room to the bar at the side of the Beach Disco. "By the way," Elizabeth said as they were waiting for their drinks, "have you seen Jess anywhere?"

"Yeah, I saw her heading for the back door a few minutes ago." Todd handed Elizabeth her root beer.

"Come to think of it, I wouldn't mind some fresh air myself," Elizabeth said.

"Sounds good to me." Todd put his arm around Elizabeth's shoulders as they took their drinks and moved toward the rear of the disco.

Elizabeth opened the rickety old wooden door that led to the beach, and they stepped outside. They were met by the sound of waves crashing against the nearby shore. A sea breeze caressed them.

"Mmmm." Todd took a deep breath. "I don't think I could ever get tired of the smell of the ocean."

"I know what you mean," Elizabeth agreed. "One good whiff and all your troubles seem to disappear." She, too, breathed deeply and lifted her face to the star-drenched, velvet-black sky.

"Speaking of trouble . . ." Todd pointed toward the steps that led down to the beach. "Here comes your sister."

Jessica's laughter flooded the night air as she approached the lights of the Beach Disco, soccer team co-captain Aaron Dallas on one arm, Neil Freemount, Sweet Valley High's newest heartthrob, on the other.

Elizabeth tactfully overlooked Todd's putdown of Jessica. Her boyfriend's less-than-enthusiastic feelings about her sister bothered Elizabeth, who was fiercely loyal to her twin, no matter what.

"Jess," Elizabeth called out happily. "Hi." She gave a big wave.

"Liz." Jessica left Aaron and Neil behind as she rushed forward to hug her twin. Then she took a step back and surveyed her sister critically. "Hey, I was looking for that skirt when I was getting dressed earlier." She fingered Elizabeth's red mini.

"Jess, I just got this. How about you give it a week or so before you decide to make it part of your own wardrobe?" She gave her sister a light tap on the arm. "Besides, your outfit looks fantastic." Jessica was wearing a pair of indigo-blue cropped pants and a matching blue-striped T-shirt. In one hand, she carried a pair of navy espadrilles.

"You think so? Well, in that case, you look pretty great yourself." Jessica giggled. "Are you having fun tonight?" she asked.

Elizabeth nodded vigorously, giving Todd a squeeze around the waist. "And you?"

65

"Don't I always?" Jessica gave her most dazzling smile. "Well, listen, I'll see you later." She slipped her espadrilles back on her feet. "I was just on my way in to dance." She looked over her shoulder. "Either of you guys interested in joining me?" Aaron and Neil readily followed her into the disco.

Inside, Jessica whirled across the dance floor, stretching, strutting, kicking her legs up, and spinning around and around. She moved gracefully from one partner to another, her silvery peals of laughter blending with The Droids' pulsing beat. Suddenly she was looking up at Winston Egbert's eager face.

"Jess, how about giving your old pal Win a twirl?"

Everyone knew that for years Winston had been madly in love with Jessica. And though Winston had recently discovered that there were other girls in the world, Jessica didn't want to risk encouraging him. Those countless years of having him at her heels were more than enough for her.

"Win, I really have to stop for a little while. I'm totally pooped." Jessica took a few steps backward.

"Well, can I get you something to drink?" Winston closed the distance Jessica had put between them.

Jessica scanned the room quickly. "Oh, there's Cara. I've barely said a word to her all night. Winston, I think I'll have to take a rain check on your offer." She hurried off before Winston had a chance to protest.

"Cara, you've got to save me from Winston." Jessica raced to her friend's side.

"Why, Jess, don't you want the honor of having the class clown dance all over your toes?" Cara snickered.

"No way," Jessica said emphatically.

"Well, I guess I can't blame you," Cara responded. "So because I'm your very best friend, I'll guard you from Win's two left feet. And what's more, I'll also tell you the very latest on Roger Barrett's mother."

"Oh, yeah? What's happening with her?" Jessica asked curiously.

"She's in a coma!" Cara announced the news as if it were her own private discovery.

"No! Poor Roger. How's he taking it?"

"Well . . . I didn't exactly talk to him," admitted Cara. "But I did hear that he's trying to find a way to fly his mother to Houston for some kind of big-deal open-heart surgery. They say it's Mrs. Barrett's only chance for survival."

"But how on earth is Roger going to find the money for that? The Barretts haven't got a single penny to their name."

Cara shrugged. "Beats me," she said.

Their conversation was interrupted by Lila Fowler, who breezed over and tapped Jessica on the shoulder. "Gee, Jess," she breathed. "I'm *so* sorry."

Jessica gave Lila a quizzical look.

"I guess it's pretty much official now," Lila continued. "My condolences."

Jessica gave Lila a hard stare. "What's official? Sorry about what?"

Lila jutted her chin in the direction of the entrance. "But maybe you already knew they'd be here."

Jessica turned around and looked. Suddenly she froze. Coming into the Beach Disco was her brother. On his arm, as if it were the most natural thing in the world, was Betsy Martin.

Steven and Betsy moved to the music, trying to avoid the haughty looks and curious glances of people around them.

"I guess he goes for women who've been around," they overheard Paul Sherwood saying to Bruce Patman. The two boys chortled loudly. Betsy blanched as she hung her head in humiliation.

"Betsy." Steven cupped his hand under her chin and tilted her head up. "Don't you pay them a bit of attention. They're not worth a second thought." His voice was strong.

Betsy met Steven's reassuring gaze. "I try not to let it get to me. Really I do. But that kind of criticism follows me everywhere I go in this town." Betsy's words rang with hurt and hopelessness. "Sometimes I think I should just pick up and go someplace where I don't know anyone. Start from the beginning again."

The Droids started to play a slow song, and

Steven ushered Betsy off the dance floor. "Running away never solved anyone's problems," he said. He found them an empty table near the bar.

Betsy was quiet for a few moments. "I guess that's true," she said finally. "My father is a champion at running away. And it only makes things worse." Her face was a mask of pain. "But it's so hard to stick around and try to make things better. I mean, what's the use of trying to change if people won't let you?" Her hazel eyes grew moist with unshed tears. "They're so cruel." Betsy sniffled.

Steven reached across the gray-slate table and squeezed her hand. "Not everyone is like that," he said softly.

"I know, Steven." Betsy brightened a little as she gazed at him. "You're not like that. In fact, you're pretty special." The corners of her mouth turned up in a shy smile.

Steven's face grew crimson with embarrassment, and he played nervously with a lock of hair. "There are lots of special people in the world," he managed to say. "You just have to look for them."

"Did I hear someone call? 'Special' is my middle name!" A tall, thin young man with curly black hair stood beside the table. His warm brown eyes were partially hidden by his thick tortoise-shell glasses.

"Jason!" Steven jumped up and clapped his friend on the back. "It's good to see you. Did you just get into town?"

Jason nodded, but his gaze was riveted on Betsy.

"Oh, Jason, this is Betsy Martin." Steven made the introductions. "This is Jason Stone, a friend of mine from college. But you can call him Mr. Special," Steven joked. "Jason's the one who's been getting all my assignments for me this week," he added.

Jason stuck his hand out awkwardly. "It's a real pleasure, Betsy."

Betsy didn't move a muscle. "Hello," she said flatly, her eyes never leaving Steven's face.

"Well—uh—maybe I'm—uh—interrupting something," Jason stammered, thrusting his hands into his pants pockets.

"No, not at all," Steven said hastily. "Please, why don't you join us?"

"Are you sure?" Jason asked politely, his gaze still on Betsy.

"Absolutely," replied Steven. He realized that Betsy was testy with strangers, but Jason was one of the sweetest guys he knew. Steven had no doubt that Betsy would soften toward his friend as soon as she got to know him.

Steven pulled a chair over to the table. Then he ordered some soft drinks. "Betsy is Tricia's sister," Steven explained as Jason sat down. He tried to keep his tone matter-of-fact, but his voice became unsteady as he spoke Tricia's name.

A look of understanding spread across Jason's face. He addressed Betsy. "I can't tell you how sorry I was to hear about your sister. My sympathies are with you."

70

Betsy gave a tiny nod. "I'll be fine," she said stiffly.

"Yes, I'm sure you will," Jason responded. "So," he added, changing the subject as their drinks were brought to the table, "you're Betsy Martin." He gave a tentative smile. "I've heard a lot about you."

Betsy's upper lip curled menacingly. "I'll bet you have," she replied bitterly. "You and everyone else."

Jason's cheeks turned crimson, and he studied the tabletop. "I—I didn't mean it that way. I meant—well, I've been phoning Steven every night to give him his assignments, and he's been telling me about you. I hear you're quite a talented artist."

Steven jumped to his friend's aid. "You see, Betsy, I've been bragging to Jason about your work. Jason's an artist, too. And a very good one," Steven added with pride.

"Oh," said Betsy. Her tone was less harsh, but she made no effort to encourage conversation. Instead, she drummed her hands noisily on the table, in time with The Droids' beat.

"Good music, huh?" Jason said.

"They're OK," replied Betsy. An uncomfortable hush fell over the threesome.

"Jason teaches a Saturday morning life-drawing class at the Valley Community Center," Steven told Betsy in a final effort to break the ice. "He comes in from school every weekend for it." Steven stirred his Coke around in his glass with a straw.

Betsy put down her drink and looked directly at Jason for the first time. Steven had obviously hit on the right thing to say about his friend. "That's *your* class?"

Jason beamed. "Uh-huh. Have you heard about it?"

Now it was Betsy's turn to blush. "Sure. My sister always used to tell me about the class. She said I should take it. But every time Saturday morning rolled around, I was too afraid," Betsy confessed.

"Why?" asked Steven. "Drawing people seems to be a specialty of yours. I'd think a life-drawing class would be just the kind of thing you'd go for."

Betsy nodded slowly. "It is. But I kept worrying about what the other students would think— a girl like me in an art class."

Jason leaned forward. "Betsy, there are all kinds of people in this class," he said kindly. "Young, old, wealthy, poor. It's for the whole community. The only requirement is that you be serious about your work—and that you enjoy it. From everything Steven tells me, you'd fit right in."

Betsy smiled at Steven, her face glowing with pleasure now. "You really said some nice things about me, didn't you?"

"And they were all true," responded Steven. "But right now I think my friend here is trying to extend an invitation to you." He carefully channeled the conversation back to Jason's art class.

"Steve's right," Jason admitted a little shyly. "I'd like it very much if you'd come tomorrow." His face was flushed, and he toyed nervously with his glasses.

Betsy looked at Jason warily. "I don't know," she began. "The other reason I was afraid was because I can't imagine drawing in a room filled with other people. When I work, it's private."

"I understand, Betsy," Jason replied. "What you put on paper can be very personal—and revealing. But eventually you've got to learn to share that part of you. That's what art is all about. It's a way of communicating." Jason's voice grew more confident as he talked about his favorite subject. It was clear that he was in his element now. "Besides," he added a bit more gently, "most of the people in class are busy concentrating on their own work. They're really there for themselves, not so that they can judge everyone around them."

Betsy's expression softened as Jason spoke, and she appeared to be considering his words. "Steve," she finally said, "what do you think?"

Steve ran his hand through his thick, dark hair. "I think it's a great idea," he answered. "And you couldn't have a better teacher." He gave Jason a little swat on the shoulder.

Betsy played with an ice cube in her glass. "Well, if you think I should, I'll give it a try."

"Fantastic!" exclaimed Jason, his face lighting up in a grin. He reached over and took

Betsy's hand. "I promise you, you won't be sorry."

Betsy instantly recoiled from his touch, and the hard look was back in her eyes. "Don't forget that this is purely a student-teacher relationship," she said, an icy edge to her voice. "It's not going any further. So you can forget all those things you've heard about me. I'm not like that anymore."

Steven rushed to Jason's defense. "Betsy, Jason didn't mean any harm. He would never take advantage of anyone. Believe me."

Jason drained his glass and put it back on the table. "Betsy," he began softly, "I don't know what you think I've heard about you, but let me assure you that I never expect anything in return for my teaching except satisfied students. You're not doing this for me—or for Steven," he added more firmly. "If you come to class, it should be because you want to work on your art. Period."

"Well, I do want to do that," Betsy said cautiously.

"Then come. And bring some samples of your work with you," Jason said. "I'd be delighted to see you."

"OK," Betsy said, but it was clear that her guard was still up. "Just once, to see what it's like."

Jason beamed.

"I'm glad that's been decided," Steven said, also smiling. "And now, may I take the opportunity to point out all these happy people dancing to the music? I think it's time to join them."

Jason and Betsy followed Steven's lead as he rose from the table and headed toward the dance floor.

Eight

"I've never been so humiliated in my whole life as I was last night at the Beach Disco," yelled Jessica. She climbed out of the Wakefield pool and raced toward Steven, who had just come out of the house and was settling into one of the yellow-and-white pool-side deck chairs.

"Jessica, I don't know what you're screaming about, but I wish you'd let me relax. It's been a hard week." Steven stretched his long legs out and opened his newspaper.

"Oh, no, you don't." Jessica lifted the paper out of her brother's hand. "We're going to talk." She grabbed a huge beach towel, wrapped it around her bikini-clad body, and sat down in a chair next to Steven's.

Steven shook his head wearily. "Sounds to me like *you* intend to do the talking, and I'm just supposed to listen. Look, Jess, I'm not up for this."

"Well, you're not making it any easier on yourself," Jessica scolded. "Or on the rest of us."

Steven sighed. There was absolutely no use in trying to stop Jessica when she had something to say. "I guess I'm not going to get any peace until I hear you out. OK, then. Spill it."

Jessica looked at her brother's drawn expression. His eyes were bloodshot, and he looked thinner. She really did feel sorry for him. Maybe, she thought, she should try a softer approach. "Steve," Jessica made her voice soothing as she changed tack as smoothly as a sailboat in a light breeze. "It's going to be tough enough getting over Tricia on your own. You really shouldn't have to deal with someone else's pain, too."

"The someone else being Betsy, I presume?"

"Yes, of course," replied Jessica, her furrowed brow the very picture of concern.

"Gee, Jess, I'm overwhelmed by your consideration for me," Steven said coolly.

"Well, what else would you expect of your very own sister?" Jessica shot Steven her most winning smile, one that worked on almost everyone.

Except her brother. "Maybe you should show a little consideration for Betsy, too," Steven replied, his voice growing tight. "Why don't you give her a break, Jessica?"

Jessica got up and paced around by the edge of the pool. "Steven, why don't you give *yourself* a break? The last thing you need right now is to be associated with someone like Betsy Martin."

"Wrong. The last thing I need is to hear another comment like that. I've had more than enough of them this week."

"Maybe there's a good reason for that." Jessica's voice rose. "Betsy Martin is bad news. And bringing her to the Beach Disco, where everyone in town can see you, is even worse. I was so ashamed, I just wanted to melt into the floor."

"Jessica, that's more than enough." Steven's tone cut through the still morning air like a knife. "Betsy's changed. That's all there is to it." His words rang with finality.

But Jessica wasn't finished. How could Steven be so blind? she thought. Betsy's checkered past could fill a book the size of Webster's dictionary. A girl like that wouldn't behave for long. "Steven, you and Liz are two of a kind—always ready to believe the best about absolutely anyone. Maybe you two should have been the twins instead of her and me." Jessica chuckled at the idea.

Steven sat up straight in his chair, anger plain on his face. "This isn't something to laugh about. Of all people, a lawyer's daughter ought to know that a person is innocent until proven guilty. And Betsy's record since she's been under our roof has been first-rate. Why don't you open up to her, Jess?"

Jessica clenched her fists. "No way," she told her brother. "Betsy Martin will never be a part of my life." With that, she stormed off toward the patio doors.

"What's with Jess?" Elizabeth had come around the path leading from the front of the house just in time to see her twin hurry off.

"Oh, I didn't want to take her sisterly advice," Steven explained as Elizabeth settled into the chair next to his.

"Let me guess," Elizabeth said, taking off her terry beach robe to reveal a simple turquoise tank suit. She stretched out in the sun. "I'll bet her advice was about Betsy."

Steven sighed. "I'm afraid so."

"Well, you know, Steve, you *have* been spending an awful lot of time with her." Elizabeth squinted over at her brother, shading her eyes with her hand.

"Oh, no," Steven groaned. "Not you, too. Liz, you and Jessica are one big case of double trouble. Why can't I just lie here and be left alone?"

Elizabeth studied her brother's sad, lonely face. "Steven, I don't want to make your life any tougher than it is right now," she said sympathetically. "It's just that I'm worried about you. And about Betsy, too. She seems so dependent on you. Steve, you're her only real companion."

Steven nodded his head. "I can't say you're wrong, Liz. But what can I do? If she needs me, I've got to be there for her."

"But, Steve, you haven't had enough time

79

alone even to begin to recover from—from what happened."

"I know. Lord, do I know." Suddenly Steven's face was in his hands, and his head rolled from side to side in grief. "I can't believe she's gone," he mumbled through his tears. "Tricia. My Trish."

Elizabeth went over to her brother and put an arm around him. She could feel his body tremble as he unleashed his tears. She sat there for several minutes, hugging him tightly until he grew calm again.

Finally Steven wiped his eyes with the corner of his towel. "That's the first time in days that I've really let my feelings out," he confessed. "I think a good cry was just what I needed."

"Well, my diagnosis is that you should probably do it more often," Elizabeth told her brother.

"OK, Doctor Wakefield, whatever you say."

"No, Steven, I'm serious." Elizabeth's voice was firm. "And you're not going to get a chance if you spend every waking moment with Betsy."

"I suppose there is something to what you're saying. When I'm with Betsy, I have to be strong enough for the two of us," Steven admitted.

"By the way," Elizabeth asked, "where *is* Betsy, anyway? I'm surprised she's not by your side right now."

"She's at Jason Stone's art class," Steven explained. "We met him last night at the Beach Disco, and he really seemed to like Betsy, even though she did everything she could to turn him off." Steven's face darkened as he recalled Betsy's harsh treatment of his friend.

"Why?" Elizabeth settled back into her own chair. "Jason's such a nice guy."

"The nicest," agreed Steven. "But to Betsy, no guy is nice. She's had such bad experiences with men, from her father on down, that she doesn't trust any of them."

"Except you," Elizabeth reminded him.

"OK, you're right," Steven admitted. "But Jason did end up convincing her to try his class. Maybe he'll win her over, too," he added hopefully.

"Maybe. Though from what I can tell, Betsy doesn't want any guy but you. And you're not doing anything to discourage her. Steven, I know you're just trying to help her, but in the long run, you're making it even worse. She must be getting the wrong idea about your feelings by now."

Steven frowned. "Liz, I can't just turn my back on her." His voice was firm.

"I'm not suggesting that you turn your back on her. I just think you should ease up. Give yourself a little room to breathe. Steven, why do you feel so totally responsible for Betsy?"

Steven's face took on a faraway look, and for several minutes he was silent. Elizabeth sensed that he was holding something back. At one point it appeared as if he was going to confide in her, but at the last moment, Steven seemed to change his mind. Finally he spoke. "Look, Liz," he said resolutely, "I appreciate your concern, but this is my business, not yours. Besides, I'm going back to school the day after tomorrow. Betsy will be without me. She'll have to learn to stand on her own two feet. And she will. She can do it." Steven leaned down and picked up his newspaper, turning to the sports section. Clearly the conversation was over.

"I hope you're right," Elizabeth said as she got up and went over to the diving board. But she couldn't help thinking about the drawing Jessica had seen of Steven in Betsy's sketch pad, right there with the pictures of Tricia and their mother. Would Steven really be that easy to forget when Monday came? Elizabeth executed a graceful swan dive into the cool water. Somehow she didn't think so.

Later that afternoon, Elizabeth was sitting on the living-room couch, reading over her latest "Eyes and Ears" column.

Make way for the champ: Winston Egbert, the Sweet Valley High junior who broke the school record for pizza-eating last week, will try to set a new world record this Thursday afternoon by eating seven extra-large pizzas in one sitting. Winston's attempt will take place at Guido's Pizzeria, and will be televised by KSVH television for the six o'clock news.

Elizabeth penciled in an additional line at the end of the paragraph. "We're rooting for you,

Winston," she wrote. Elizabeth went on to the next item.

Are his days of playing the field almost over? T.H., handsome Sweet Valley High senior, was spotted at the Beach Disco Saturday night, pursuing a certain ravishing blond singer. Is it possible that the popular man-about-campus is succumbing to D.L.'s irresistible charms?

Elizabeth chuckled as she recalled the way Tim Houseman had been hanging onto Dana Larson's every note the previous night. And Dana hadn't minded in the least. They made a good couple, Elizabeth decided as she heard the front door open. She looked up to see Betsy enter the room.

"Hi, how was art class?" Elizabeth asked cheerfully.

Betsy sank into one of the beige armchairs across from the couch and crossed her long legs. "Don't even ask," she said.

Elizabeth put down her pencil and the typed pages. "Why not? Betsy, what happened?"

"Nothing I shouldn't have expected," Betsy said cryptically. "But for some reason I thought this time would be different."

"I don't understand," Elizabeth said. "Different from what?"

"I thought this time I could trust someone, but I was wrong. Dumb me. Stupid, stupid me," Betsy berated herself.

"Betsy, what went on today?" Art class was the one place Elizabeth had figured Betsy would be totally comfortable. What could have gone wrong?

"Liz, you don't have to listen to my problems," Betsy told her. "They would bore you." She slumped further into her seat.

"Try me," Elizabeth said softly.

Betsy sighed. "It's the story of my life. Everything was fine, but—" she stopped in midsentence.

"But what?"

"But Jason Stone turned out to be a creep, just like every other guy. He was only out to get one thing from me." Betsy's words tumbled out in a tearful rush. "I was so excited to be there, surrounded by people who love to paint and draw as much as I do. And Jason really liked the work I showed him. He was so enthusiastic—or at least he pretended to be. 'Betsy, these are wonderful,' he kept telling me. I should have figured out right then and there what he was after. But no. I really let myself think that someone believed in me, that I had talent. And he kept coming around during class to encourage me. I was on top of the world. And then—and then, Liz, he asked me out." Betsy's hands trembled in her lap, and she stared straight ahead.

Elizabeth waited patiently for the rest of the story, but Betsy remained silent. Was that the whole explanation? Jason's interest in her was the cause of Betsy's anxiety? "I'm afraid I don't understand," Elizabeth said. "What's wrong with Jason's asking a beautiful, talented girl out on a date?"

"Elizabeth, a date with Betsy Martin means one thing, and one thing only." Betsy's voice was hard. "Or hasn't the star gossip columnist heard the dirt on me?" Her hazel eyes blazed with hurt and anger. "And I thought Betsy Martin stories were a dime a dozen."

Elizabeth bit down on her lip to keep from crying out in frustration. She was trying her hardest to be a friend to Betsy, but it required endless patience and understanding. Elizabeth wondered if she'd ever make any real headway with the girl, or if it would always be two steps forward and three steps back.

"Look, Betsy," Elizabeth said finally, her voice sympathetic, "I think you're wrong about Jason. He's a lovely, sweet guy. He probably just wants a chance to talk with you over dinner, or take you to the movies. What's more," she added lightly, "I think he has very good taste."

But Elizabeth might just as well have addressed her compliment to a brick wall. Betsy jumped up out of her chair, hands on hips as she faced Elizabeth. "Maybe that's the way it is when a boy asks *you* out. But it's never been that way for me. I don't know why I expected you to understand." Betsy stalked away.

I certainly missed the mark that time, Elizabeth thought sadly, after Betsy had left the room.

Listlessly she picked up her "Eyes and Ears" column and ran her index finger down the page, until she found the place where she'd left off earlier. *I can fill a whole article with tidbits about Sweet Valley High*, she thought as she stared at the typed pages. *But the real drama is going on right under my own roof!*

Nine

"Bruce Patman's father is doing what!?" Jessica screeched.

Next to her, Steven put his hands over his ears. "Why don't you scream a little louder, Jess? Maybe Mr. Patman will hear you and come all the way over to tell you the news in person."

Jessica turned a disgusted face on her brother. "Ha-ha," she said scathingly. "I wasn't talking to you, anyway. I was talking to Liz."

"Oh, sorry, Jessica." Steven gave his sister a labored grin as he drowned his pancakes with maple syrup. "In that case, I'm sorry for listening in."

"Come on, kids," Mrs. Wakefield said sharply. "It's Sunday morning. Can't we have a little peace around here?" She reached for the coffee-pot.

"Sure, Mom," Jessica answered, pausing to

take a big gulp of freshly squeezed orange juice. "Just as soon as Liz explains what Mr. Bigwig Patman is up to this time."

The Wakefields and Betsy were gathered around the kitchen table for the weekly family brunch. The sun streamed in through the open windows, and outside, the birds chirped cheerfully. It was another picture-perfect Sweet Valley morning.

"Well, Liz?" Jessica tapped impatiently on her sister's plate with a fork. While she was at it, she speared Elizabeth's last bite of sausage and popped it into her mouth.

"It's just the way I told you already," said Elizabeth. "Mr. Patman has offered to pay for Roger Barrett's mother's operation."

"I just can't believe it!" Jessica exclaimed.

"It's true. Enid and George ran into Olivia last night, and she told them. Mrs. Barrett's in Houston at the hospital already, and they've scheduled her surgery for this afternoon."

"Why in the world would Mr. Patman pay Mrs. Barrett's medical expenses?" Jessica was still incredulous. "I'd think the Barretts would be the last kind of people Bruce and his father would bother with." She shook her head in puzzlement and disbelief.

"You never know about people." Betsy spoke up for the first time. "Sometimes you'd be surprised by their attention and kindness. I mean, I never dreamed that one day I'd be sitting here having brunch with all of you." Her eyes were fixed on Steven's face as she talked.

Jessica gave Elizabeth a swift kick under the table, as if to say, "I told you so." It was plain to both of them that Betsy's moody and withdrawn frame of mind following the previous day's art class had disappeared, thanks to Steven's presence.

"Betsy has a point," put in Ned Wakefield. "Generosity is a matter of temperament, not the amount of money someone has. But from what I know of Henry Wilson Patman, he *is* a rather unlikely candidate for this kind of big-heartedness."

Elizabeth nodded. "If he's anything like his son, that's true," she said. "But I guess Roger is thankful for his help—whatever the reason behind it is."

"Maybe," Jessica answered. "Although I think there's more to this than meets the eye." She finished her juice. "But I don't have time to talk about it right now. I told Neil Freemount I'd meet him for a game of tennis after breakfast. Mom, Dad, can I be excused now?" Jessica was on her feet without waiting for an answer. As she disappeared from view, the doorbell rang. "I'll get it on my out," Jessica yelled from the other room.

Elizabeth heard her twin banging around in the hall closet, where they kept their tennis rackets. Then she heard Jessica open the front door. "Hi," said a male voice. It sounded vaguely familiar, but Elizabeth couldn't place it.

"Hi. Steve's in the kitchen." Elizabeth could

just make out what her sister was saying. "You can find your way, can't you?"

Elizabeth saw Betsy freeze, her juice glass clutched in her hand, her knuckles white. Elizabeth put two and two together. The voice belonged to Jason Stone!

A few seconds later Jason's tall, thin figure appeared in the kitchen doorway. "Oh, I'm sorry." He blushed apologetically. "I didn't expect to catch you in the middle of a meal."

"Jason! Hey, it's OK," replied Steven. "We're just finishing up. Why don't you sit down with us and have a cup of coffee? I think you know my sister, Liz, and of course, Betsy."

As he looked at Betsy, Jason blushed even more furiously. "Hi, Betsy," he managed timidly. But Betsy said nothing.

"Nice to see you, Jason." Elizabeth greeted him with what she hoped was enough cheerfulness for both her and Betsy.

"Hi, Liz." Jason smiled shyly.

"And these are my parents," Steven said.

Jason went over and shook hands with Mr. and Mrs. Wakefield, who were just getting up from the table.

"Jason, hello. Steven's told us so many lovely things about you," said Alice Wakefield.

"Yes, nice to meet you," added Ned Wakefield. "Even if it's just for a moment. Alice and I have to rush off to a meeting of the school board, but you're welcome to make yourself comfortable." He motioned to Jessica's empty seat.

"Thank you," Jason said, lowering his lanky body into the chair. "I *would* love a cup of coffee, if it's OK with everyone." He cast a sidelong glance at Betsy, who remained silent. Steven got up and took a mug from the cupboard while his parents bid everyone goodbye and left the kitchen. He filled the mug and handed it to Jason.

"Thanks, Steve," said Jason. Then he turned to Betsy. "I really just came by to drop this off." He held out her sketch pad, which he had been carrying under his arm. "You—uh—ran out of class so quickly yesterday, you forgot to take your drawings with you."

Betsy leaned across the table. "Thank you," she mumbled, taking the pad and putting it under her seat.

"Betsy, I want you to know that I meant what I said yesterday. You've done some very fine work."

"Sure," Betsy said flatly, picking at an imaginary piece of lint on her blue sweat shirt.

"No, I'm absolutely serious." Jason was emphatic. "As a matter of fact, I was wondering whether you've ever considered applying to art school." He added cream to his coffee while he spoke. "I don't mean one class a week. I mean training with professionals. Every day. To become a professional." Betsy looked up suspiciously. "You really could be great," Jason concluded, his nervousness giving way to excitement.

Elizabeth held her breath as Betsy digested

Jason's words. "Well, what if I *were* interested?" Betsy asked guardedly after a few moments. "I wouldn't have any idea where to begin." She eyed Jason coolly.

"Betsy, at this very moment, the Los Angeles Academy of Fine Arts is conducting a talent search." Now that he had gotten going, Jason's words came out in an exhilarated rush. "The three people they choose will get four years of free tuition, room, and board. And L.A. Academy is one of the best art schools in the country!"

Elizabeth could see Betsy's icy facade begin to melt. "Really?" Betsy asked, a note of interest surfacing in her voice.

Jason grinned broadly at her response. "Really," he replied.

"Oh, but I could never be good enough for L.A." Betsy's face darkened.

"Of course you could. You might be one of the people they're looking for. No kidding," Jason said, his voice sincere.

"It sounds terrific," Steven put in. "How do you enter the competition?"

"Good question," said Betsy, all her attention on Steven. "I'll bet you have to have all kinds of experience."

"Actually, you don't. It's a pretty simple procedure," explained Jason. "You have to fill out a short application and then submit a portfolio of fifteen of your best works. That's all. Only trouble is, they're reviewing the final applications right now. But, Betsy," Jason said, watching her intently, "an old teacher of mine is head

of the admissions board. If I call him, he'll probably agree to accept one more application."

Some of the sparkle went out of Betsy's eyes.
"In return for what?" she asked. "It had to be
too good to be true."

"In return for knowing you really want to get
in," Jason replied.

Elizabeth was impressed by the extraordinary
patience and tenderness he projected.

"This could be the best thing that ever happened to you," Jason added.

"Well, of course I want it," Betsy told Jason
warily. "It would be like a dream come true.
But just for starters, I don't even have a portfolio to show."

"Oh, that's no problem." Jason stirred a spoon
around in his coffee mug. "You've got at least
fifteen first-rate drawings in your sketch pad
alone. All we have to do is select and arrange
them."

"*We!*" Betsy exclaimed.

Elizabeth cringed at the seething resentment
in that one word.

"Well, yes, I, uh—I thought maybe—um—we
could get together this evening before I leave
for school, and I could—ah—help you put your
portfolio together. . . ." Jason's voice trailed off,
and his face grew red.

Betsy pushed her chair away from the table
and jumped up. "Well, you can stop thinking
anything of the kind, Jason Stone. I knew it
wasn't my drawing. I knew all you were after
was a night alone with me. And when you had

93

gotten what you wanted, it would have been, 'Oh, I'm so sorry. My teacher says they can't take any more applicants. I tried, really I did . . .' " Betsy mimicked. "Well, you can save your lies for somebody else." She turned on her heel and ran out of the kitchen.

An embarrassed silence filled the air. Finally Steven spoke up. "Jason, don't take it to heart. Betsy's had it incredibly rough." He explained a little about Betsy's background. "So you see," he finished, "she has a hard time learning to trust people, especially men."

Jason nodded. "I understand. But, Steve, she seems so open with you. When she was dancing with you Friday night, she was so happy and lovely that—well, to tell you the truth, I just couldn't keep my eyes off her," he admitted bashfully. "What's your secret?" Elizabeth noted a twinge of envy in his voice.

Now the heat rushed to Steven's face.

"I think," Elizabeth helped her brother out, "that Steven was there for Betsy when she needed him most. That and the fact that he loved Tricia as much as he did." Elizabeth took Steven's hand and gave it a supportive squeeze as she spoke Tricia's name. They were silent for a few moments, absorbed in their memories.

"But, Jason—don't lose heart," Steven finally told his friend softly. "Betsy'll come around. At least I hope so. The fact of the matter is that I'm kind of worried about her." Steven took a sip of his coffee. "One day she's fine—nice to everyone around the house, helpful, more together than I've ever seen her before, even though she's hurting incredibly inside. Then she just seems to explode, almost for no reason at all." Steven echoed Elizabeth's thoughts. "She's under so much stress right now," he continued, "between her sister and her father. . . . Well, she doesn't talk about it much, but you can tell it's tearing her apart. And she vents all her tension and frustration and misery on other people." Steven shook his head. "But I think she's really a good person underneath the rough exterior."

"I sense that," Jason agreed. "You can tell just by looking at her drawings. She treats her subjects with real tenderness and intelligence."

"Well, just give her time, time and patience," Steven concluded.

"I've got plenty of both of those," Jason reflected a little sadly. "But, meanwhile"—he pointed underneath the chair where Betsy had been sitting—"why doesn't one of you bring her the sketch pad. I think Betsy's seen enough of me for today."

Steven reached down for the pad. "I'll take it to her," he said.

Elizabeth leaned over and grabbed his arm. "No, don't," she proposed, the beginnings of a plan taking shape in her head. "Jason," she asked, excitement surfacing in her voice, "do you really think Betsy's good enough for the L.A. Academy?"

"Yes, of course," replied Jason. "I meant every word I said. But why do you ask, Liz? We can't make Betsy apply if she's decided against it."

"Yes and no," Elizabeth said, a gleam coming into her blue-green eyes. "You say there are enough pictures right in that pad to fill a portfolio?"

Jason nodded slowly, understanding spreading across his face. He broke into a broad grin. "Liz, you're brilliant."

Elizabeth gave a dazzling smile. "It's not a bad idea, is it?"

"Hey, wait a minute, you two." Steven's brow was furrowed. "How come I feel like I'm missing something?"

Elizabeth turned toward her brother. "Look, Steve. We know Betsy would give anything to go to a serious art school, right?"

"Right."

"And we also know she's got a good chance of getting in, even if she doesn't think so."

"Uh-huh."

"Well, just suppose somebody else were to enter Betsy in the L.A. Academy competition. . . ."

"Yes." Now Steven, too, began to grin. "Just suppose. . . ." Pleased with the idea, Steven lifted his coffee cup in the air. "I propose a toast," he declared, "to the L.A. Academy. And to Betsy Martin."

The three touched their mugs together. "To Betsy," Jason and Elizabeth chimed in happily.

Ten

Steven hoisted his knapsack on his back. "How come I feel as if I'm forgetting something?" he wondered aloud as his family and Betsy gathered in the living room to say goodbye to him.

"You have all your school books?" asked his father. Steven nodded. "Even that microeconomics text?" A teasing smile crept across Ned Wakefield's handsome features. Microeconomics class had given Steven more than his share of headaches that semester—due largely to a professor who, Steven claimed, could put sleeping-pill manufacturers out of business in five minutes flat.

"Don't remind me." Steven groaned. "That's where I'll be first thing tomorrow morning, textbook in hand." He patted his knapsack to indicate that the book was tucked away inside.

"How about those new jeans I bought you?"

Alice Wakefield asked from her seat on the couch. "Do you have those?"

"Yes, I do, Mom. And the shirts, too," answered Steven. "So I guess that *is* everything." But he sounded unsure, and somehow empty. "At least everything I can bring with me, now," Steven added sadly.

On his face was the faraway expression that Elizabeth had seen so often in the past week. She realized her brother was thinking about Tricia again. It was no wonder he seemed empty, no wonder he felt as if he'd forgotten something. He was returning to school without Tricia's loving goodbye kiss, without the knowledge that she'd be waiting eagerly for his next visit home, without the comfort of her sweet smile. Steven might have everything he was supposed to have packed up in his knapsack, but Elizabeth knew that her brother had a hollow spot in his heart. She moved toward him and put a hand on his arm. "Are you going to be OK up at school?" she asked softly.

Steven nodded. "The best thing I could possibly do right now is to throw myself into my schoolwork—Lord knows I have enough catching up to do. Maybe I'll be too busy to think about . . . well, about anything else," Steven said, making his voice strong. "But thanks for asking, Liz." He threw his arms around her and gave her a hug. "You take care," he said. Then, lowering his voice so she alone could hear, he added, "And either Jason or I will call if anything happens with the big plan."

"OK," Elizabeth said enthusiastically. "I'm keeping my fingers crossed."

"What are you keeping your fingers crossed for, Liz?" Jessica had sidled up to them to claim her piece of Steven's attention.

Steven gave her an affectionate squeeze. "She's crossing her fingers that you won't get into any trouble before my next visit home," he joked.

Jessica gave her shiny blond hair a toss. "Trouble? Me?" She adopted a tone of pure innocence.

Steven laughed. "Yes, you. I think they had you in mind when they invented the word. But try to toe the line until I get back, will you?" He dealt her a playful punch on the arm.

"Aye-aye, sir." Jessica gave a mock salute.

Then Steven embraced his mother. "See you soon," he said.

Alice Wakefield gave him a kiss. "You know you're welcome whenever you need a home-cooked meal and some tender loving care," she told her son.

"Thanks, Mom," said Steven. "I'm sure I'll be taking you up on that."

"Good luck with everything, Steve," put in Ned Wakefield. He clasped his son's hand in his and held it, his dark, caring eyes mirrored by Steven's.

Finally, it was Betsy's turn to say goodbye. She flung her arms around Steven's neck and looked up at his handsome face. "Steve, I wish you didn't have to go." She sighed.

Elizabeth felt Jessica nudge her in the ribs. At

the same time, she saw her parents exchange a worried look. So they had noticed what was going on, also, Elizabeth noted.

"Betsy," Steven began. "I've got to get back to my classes and try to go on with the rest of my life—the way it was before . . ." He left his sentence unfinished.

Betsy continued to cling to Steven. "But maybe you need a few more days at home first," she suggested.

"No." Steven was firm but gentle. "The longer I wait to go back to school, the harder it will be. Besides, Trish wouldn't have wanted me to sit at home feeling sorry for myself."

At the mention of her sister's name, Betsy loosened her grasp on Steven and took a small step back. "When you put it that way," she said unhappily, "I can't argue."

Steven touched her cheek. "Betsy, don't look so sad. I'll just be a phone call away. OK?"

Betsy swallowed hard. "OK, Steve." She forced a weak smile.

"You can get in touch with me any time you want to," Steven offered.

Betsy's smile grew wider. "You mean it?"

Steven nodded. Then he gave one final wave of his hand and disappeared out the front door.

"Jessica Wakefield, maybe you'd like to come down to earth for a moment and tell the class how many electrons there are in the outer shell of an oxygen atom."

Jessica snapped to attention as she heard Mr. Russo call her name. "Um—uh—is it four?" she asked, holding her breath and praying her guess would be correct. As far as she was concerned, there was no worse way to start the week then by getting caught unprepared in Bob Russo's chemistry class. It wasn't for nothing that Mr. Russo was known as the toughest teacher at Sweet Valley High.

Now he stood in front of her desk, one hand on his hip, the other fingering a piece of chalk. Jessica cringed. She knew what was coming next.

"No, it is *not* four, Jessica," Mr. Russo bellowed, leaning over her desktop. "Would you care to make another guess?"

"Six?" Jessica whispered nervously.

"Please speak up, Jessica. I'm sure Susan and Dawn, passing notes all the way in the back row, can't hear you." The teacher gave a pointed look in their direction, and the two girls sat up guiltily. Susan Stewart quickly folded the paper and dropped it into her bookbag. Mr. Russo refocused his attention on Jessica. "Yes, Jessica? We're waiting."

Darn him! thought Jessica. *Picking on me for no reason at all.* So what if she didn't know about a dumb old atom. What difference did it make, anyway? She looked up at Mr. Russo. "Six," she said more loudly.

"Six what, Jessica?" questioned the dark, heavy-set teacher.

"I said I thought there were six electrons in

the outer shell of an oxygen atom," Jessica nearly shouted. Elizabeth always said that Mr. Russo was as fair as he was tough, but Jessica didn't believe it.

Mr. Russo chuckled. "OK, Jessica." His tone was a bit less harsh. "You guessed right. Next time, try to do your daydreaming on your own time. I've been talking about the oxygen atom all period. If you'd been listening for the past forty minutes, you wouldn't have had any trouble answering my question. Now, Emily," Mr. Russo turned his attention to the petite, dark-haired drummer for The Droids. He walked across the room to where she sat. "Can you cite some of oxygen's more important properties?"

Jessica let out a sigh of relief. Mr. Russo was finished with her. As Emily answered the teacher's questions, Jessica sneaked a glance at Elizabeth, who was seated next to her. Elizabeth flashed her twin a sympathetic smile.

Next, Mr. Russo went over to Roger Barrett. "Roger, what are the six elements crucial to human life?"

"Hydrogen, oxygen, carbon . . ." Roger began reeling off the names as easily as if he were reciting the alphabet. When he was finished, he described the atomic structure of each element, just for good measure.

Jessica listened in wonder. How could Roger be so interested in a stupid science class? Especially with his mother fighting for her life in a Houston hospital. Before the period had started, Jessica had heard him tell Elizabeth that his mother's recovery after the operation was disturbingly slow. The dark circles under Roger's eyes and the sad, drawn expression on his face attested to the fact that he had been up all night, worrying.

Jessica studied Roger out of the corner of her eye. He wasn't bad looking, despite the worn, patched pants and faded shirt. His shaggy brown hair framed a strong face, and his athlete's build was apparent even under his loose clothes. Too bad, Jessica thought, that he didn't have a penny to his name. Otherwise, he might well be high on her list of desirable boys.

"Jess!" Suddenly she was jolted out of her thoughts of Roger as her sister hissed her name and gave her a sharp poke. She looked up. Mr. Russo was heading their way.

Jessica groaned inwardly. Hadn't Mr. Russo harassed her enough for one day? But before he made it to their side of the room, the welcome sound of the bell filled the large, sunny classroom. Notebooks were slammed shut, pens and pencils quickly put away.

"On Friday there'll be a quiz on the biochemestry chapter in your textbook," Mr. Russo announced above the rising din of students' chatter.

Jessica pushed her chair away from her desk and gathered her things. "See you later, Liz," she said, quickly heading for the door and leaving all thoughts of atomic structure, Mr. Russo, and Roger Barrett behind her.

*   *   *

"*You* ask him, Cara," prodded Lila Fowler. She plucked a blade of grass and began chewing on one end of it.

"Why me?" Cara wailed. "Bruce Patman has never even stopped to give me the time of day."

"Well, I certainly can't ask him," Lila said. "His family and mine are having another one of their famous run-ins."

The feud between the Patmans, with their old money, and the Fowlers, with their new money, was a common topic of conversation around Sweet Valley. The Fowlers were always pushing for modernization; they wanted to install the most advanced computer system in the town hall and build a huge glass-and-steel office-building complex near the mall, while the Patmans were constantly working to keep every stone in Sweet Valley exactly as it had been for the past century. Some people in town sided with Lila's family, others with Bruce's, while a third faction, which included Ned and Alice Wakefield, tried to rally for a happy medium with Sweet Valley's best interests in mind.

"What about you, Jess? Why don't you ask him?" Cara gave her best friend an imploring stare.

"No way," answered Jessica. "Don't look at me. You know my history with Bruce."

Bruce and Jessica had dated briefly, and the romance had ended badly. The two were still not on the best of terms.

Cara sighed. "Looks like I'm elected to do the dirty work for you two again."

"Honestly, Cara. You don't have to be so dramatic." Jessica rolled her big, blue-green eyes skyward. "You know you're at least as curious as we are. I mean, Mr. Patman can't be helping the Barretts simply out of the goodness of his heart."

"You can say that again," echoed Lila. "So how about it, Cara?"

"Well . . . OK," Cara agreed slowly. "I *would* like to find out what's behind this story. But you guys have to come with me."

"OK," Jessica and Lila consented. They followed Cara across the Sweet Valley High lawn to where Bruce Patman stood under the shade of a large oak tree, swinging his right arm across his well-muscled chest, making various tennis swings as he talked to Paul Sherwood.

The girls drew close to Paul and Bruce. Cara cleared her throat loudly to signal their presence.

Bruce looked over at them, finishing a flashy imaginary serve. "Well, it looks like we've got an audience," he said to Paul. "And what can we do for you lovely ladies to brighten your day?"

Jessica nudged Cara forward. "Bruce, we—uh—heard your father did something really generous." Cara heaped on the praise in her most honey-sweet voice. "You must be awfully proud of him."

Jessica was impressed with her friend's approach. *I couldn't have been more diplomatic myself*, she thought. *Cara has certainly picked up some of my best tricks*, she congratulated herself.

"Well, it goes without saying that I'm proud of him," Bruce replied in his usual arrogant manner. "I'm *always* proud of my father. That's what it means to be a Patman."

"Yes, of course," Cara said quickly. "But this seems like a kind of strange favor for your father to be doing."

"Oh, now I get it," Bruce drawled. "You three are just aching to find out what my father stands to gain by helping out Roger's mother. Is that it?" He tilted his head questioningly.

"Well, people do wonder," Jessica put in.

"Yes, people do, Jessica, especially certain people." A haughty smile flitted across Bruce's handsome face. "And I could send those people away without an answer if I wanted to." He chuckled, and Paul Sherwood also laughed. "But I won't," Bruce continued self-importantly. "I'm too much of a gentleman to keep you in suspense."

Right, thought Jessica cynically. *Bruce Patman, gentleman of the decade.* If she hadn't been so curious, she would have told him off right then and there. She gritted her teeth and remained silent.

"So there *is* a reason for your father's generosity," Cara prompted.

"My father is naturally bighearted," Bruce said loftily. "But as a matter of fact, Mrs. Barrett used to work for him on the assembly line at Patman Canning." He folded his arms. "How about that?"

"Oh, come on, Bruce." Lila waved her hand

in a gesture of disbelief, a pair of slender gold bracelets on her wrist glinting in the bright, midday sun. "According to my father, Linda Barrett worked for Patman Canning Company before Roger was even born. Isn't this a little late for favors from the boss?" Lila played offense in the latest round of the Patman-Fowler feud.

"Lila, I know your father can't be bothered with other people's problems," Bruce retaliated, "but there is such a thing as watching out for the little people."

"The little people?" Jessica spat out in disgust. She couldn't keep quiet for a second longer. "What right do you have to label anyone a little person?"

"Hey, don't get so excited, Jessica," Bruce said. "You know what I mean. In fact, your family's doing sort of the same kind of thing mine is—taking care of that girl and letting her live in your house and everything."

Jessica felt her face grow hot. Why couldn't Bruce just leave Betsy out of this?

"Of course, nobody's planning on having Roger and his mother actually move in with us," Bruce went on. "And thank goodness for that." He and Paul chortled loudly, and even Lila giggled.

Fury shot through Jessica like a rocket leaving the launch pad. They were laughing at her expense! And all because of Betsy Martin. It wasn't fair. It wasn't even her own fault. Of all the families in Sweet Valley, she, Jessica Wakefield, had to get stuck with one that opened its doors to any stray animal that happened to walk by. She had told Elizabeth that it would come down to this, that she'd be the laughingstock of the school. But did Elizabeth care? No. Some wild tramp was more important to her than her own twin sister.

The conversation continued around Jessica, with Bruce insisting that his father's generosity to Mrs. Barrett was purely noble, while Cara and Lila probed for another explanation. But Jessica was no longer interested. What did she care about Mr. Patman's intentions when her own world was being ruined by Betsy Martin?

As the three girls ambled back across the rolling green lawn with no more news about Bruce's father than they'd had before, Jessica made a resolution to herself. She would get Betsy out of her life if it was the last thing she did.

Eleven

The parking lot of Guido's Pizzeria was filling up quickly by the time Elizabeth and Todd pulled up in Todd's comfortably worn Datsun. The KSVH van was sitting out in front of the low, stucco-faced building, its back doors wide open as the news crew unloaded cameras, microphones, and other equipment. Elizabeth watched Nicholas and Regina Morrow disappear into Guido's side entrance, while Olivia Davidson and Enid climbed out of Mrs. Rollins's little blue hatchback at the other end of the lot.

"Enid! Olivia!" Elizabeth poked her head out of the car window and yelled to her friends. "Save us some seats inside, all right?"

Enid made a thumbs-up sign. "OK," she shouted back. "And if Winston doesn't have the pizza ovens all blocked up for the next year and a half, how about splitting a Guido's deluxe?"

"Sounds great," Elizabeth called as her friends headed for the pizzeria door.

Todd circled around until he found an empty space right next to the black Porsche with license plates proclaiming "1BRUCE1."

"Can you believe it!" Todd exclaimed. "Bruce Patman is joining the commoners at Guido's for the big event."

"Oh, I'm not surprised," returned Elizabeth as she let herself out the passenger door. "If there's a crowd to strut in front of, you can be sure Bruce'll turn up, especially if there are TV cameras."

Todd put his arm around her as they walked toward the entrance. "I suppose you're right," he said. "But I wouldn't expect Bruce to show up here. I mean, after that time your sister let him have a pizza right in the face, I figured he'd never come back to this place."

Elizabeth giggled as she remembered Sweet Valley High's most sought-after senior covered with pepperoni pie. "He certainly had it coming," she said, referring to the messy end to her sister's much-talked-about, but short-lived, relationship with Bruce.

"I have to admit that even I was rooting for your sister during that battle," Todd confessed. "But it *was* a long time ago. I guess Bruce is ready to visit the scene of the crime again."

They reached the entrance to Guido's, and a rich, pungent aroma surrounded them as they stepped inside the noisy restaurant. Most of the tables and booths were already taken, and people lined the swivel stools at the long white counter as well. In the center of the room, one table was empty, roped off and awaiting the arrival of the Starch King. On it, Frank DeLuna, Guido's manager, was setting down a large pitcher of ice water and a tall glass.

Elizabeth scanned the crowd until she saw Enid and Olivia at a large booth near the artificial waterfall that cascaded down Guido's rear wall. With them were John Pfeifer, sports editor for *The Oracle*, beautiful, dark-haired Annie Whitman, one of Sweet Valley High's newest cheerleaders, and her boyfriend, Ricky Capaldo, the shy manager of the cheering squad.

Enid caught Elizabeth's eye and waved. Elizabeth and Todd walked to the table, exchanging greetings and slaps on the back with other kids from school.

"Hey, Todd," called Jim Daly, teammate on the basketball team. "Looks like Winston's drawing a bigger crowd than our last game, huh?"

Todd gave an exaggerated shrug. "What can you do? Maybe we should get Winston to try his next record-breaking stunt at halftime," he shouted back as he and Elizabeth edged their way to the rear of the room.

"Hey, gang," Todd called as they approached the table.

"Hi, everyone. Think we fit?" Elizabeth asked.

"Oh, sure," answered Annie Whitman cheerfully. "Come squeeze in here." She and Ricky moved to the inside of the booth. Elizabeth and Todd crowded in beside them.

"We ordered a deluxe," Enid informed them, "but it's going to take awhile because of all these people." She made a sweeping gesture around the pizzeria.

Most people were still streaming in the door. Among them, Elizabeth had spotted her sister, sporting the new, low-back, turquoise T-shirt dress she had conned her mother into getting for her at Foxy Mama's. With her was Neil Freemount: tall, blond, impossibly cute, and grinning happily at his pretty companion. Jessica looked rather content herself, Elizabeth noted.

"Interesting," Todd remarked quietly to his girlfriend as he followed her gaze. "They've been spending a lot of time together lately, haven't they?"

Elizabeth nodded. "But it's strange. Jess has hardly said a word about him. Usually when she's got her eye on a new guy, she can't talk about anything else."

But Elizabeth quickly forgot about her sister and Neil as Winston strode into the pizza parlor, heralded by cheers, catcalls, and applause. True to form, a goofy gold-foil crown was perched on his head, the word *starch* spelled out in red cardboard letters on the points of the crown. He waved his arms high above his head, flashing a lopsided grin into the TV cameras that had been set up at the end of the counter.

As Winston slipped into his chair, Frank DeLuna slid the long, wooden-handled pizza bat into the brick oven and pulled out a large, steaming pie. He placed it on a tray and carried it over to the center table to cool off.

"Mmm! Looks so good I could eat seven of them," Winston quipped. There was laughter all around. He filled his glass with water and patted the stack of napkins at his elbow as if to ready himself for the event.

Anna Scarpelli, an anchorwoman for KSVH, stepped forward, microphone in hand. "How do you feel, Mr. Egbert?" she asked.

"Hungry," came the answer. The crowd roared. Winston was in his element. The bigger the audience, the better.

"Do you really think you'll be able to break the world record?" questioned the newscaster.

"I skipped lunch just for the occasion," Winston told her. More enthusiastic laughter filled the room.

"Here's to the Starch King," a short, dark-haired boy yelled, raising his paper cup to toast Winston's attempt.

"Long may he reign," Annie Whitman sang out in her best cheerleader voice, raising her cup, too.

"Thank you. Thank you," Winston shouted, as scores of cups were lifted in his direction. "And, now, as most of you already know," he announced, "I will attempt to break the world record by eating seven extra-large pizza pies in one sitting. So with no further ado—because it's way past my lunchtime—I shall begin." Calmly Winston picked up the first slice and began to eat it. Meanwhile, Frank DeLuna set Winston's next two pies on the counter.

"Do you think he can do it?" Enid asked as Winston reached for slice number two.

"He's certainly been practicing enough," John Pfeifer commented.

"Well, maybe practice makes perfect in sports," Olivia Davidson put in, "but in Win's case, practice might just be giving him a stomach ache. In fact," she added in a confidential whisper, "I happen to know he hasn't been feeling so great recently."

"Oh, no. You're kidding." Elizabeth groaned. "Who'd you hear that from?"

"Winston told Roger a couple of days ago," explained Olivia.

"By the way, where is Roger?" Elizabeth asked with concern. She knew his mother's illness was taking a particularly hard toll on him.

Olivia fidgeted with the purple scarf that covered her frizzy brown hair. "I'm trying not to think about it, but Mrs. Barrett's gotten worse," she said hoarsely, her big, dark eyes growing moist. "So Mr. Patman arranged for Roger to fly to Houston to be with her. He's home packing now."

"Oh, Liv, I'm so sorry," commiserated Elizabeth. The others at the table murmured their sympathies as well.

"Yeah, it's rough on him—especially after his father left him." Olivia shook her head, her dangling silver earrings swinging back and forth. "His mother's the only family he has left."

114

"But he's got you," Enid reminded her softly.

Olivia blushed a becoming shade of pink. "Yes, I'll do whatever I can for him."

"So will Bruce's father, it seems," Todd remarked.

"It does appear that way," Olivia confirmed. "Roger and I can't figure it out, but we're grateful to him."

"I can imagine," said Todd.

A dark silence hung over the group for a moment. Finally Olivia spoke again. "But I'm sure Roger wouldn't want us worrying about him in the middle of all this." She gestured with her chin in Winston's direction.

Everyone watched as he polished off the last slice of the first pie. "Will you look at him go!" exclaimed Elizabeth.

Winston leaned back in his chair and patted his stomach. "Frank, that was delicious," he wisecracked. "Can I have another one?"

"My pleasure," Frank DeLuna responded, setting the second pizza in front of Winston.

"It does look good," John Pfeifer observed. "I wish our pizza would come." With his gaze, he followed a waiter in a red-and-white-striped jacket, who made his way through the crowd to deliver a sizzling pie to DeeDee Gordon and surfer Bill Chase at a table near the jukebox.

"Patience, John, patience," Todd advised.

"How can I be patient when I'm watching Win go through one pizza after another?" John complained.

Everyone laughed, the bleak mood over Roger's mother forgotten for the time being.

"I'm sure Winston wouldn't mind letting you help him out," Elizabeth said and giggled. "He's got enough food there for the entire Sweet Valley High football team." She motioned to the counter, where pies three through five were cooling off.

Winston was in the middle of his fourth pie when the pizza John had been dreaming about was brought to the table, loaded with peppers, sausages, mushrooms, and every other ingredient in Guido's kitchen. Winston, of course, had opted for a plainer version.

Elizabeth folded her slice over lengthwise and bit into the rich, cheese-covered pie. "Ho-hot," she gasped, fluttering her hand back and forth in front of her mouth. She always promised herself she'd wait a few minutes to take that first bite so she wouldn't burn the roof of her mouth, but whenever the pizza arrived, fresh from Guido's oven, she was tempted to bite into it as soon as possible.

Todd wagged his finger playfully. "I thought you told me you were going to let it cool down a little this time. Like I do." He made a big show of blowing on his pizza several times and letting it sit for a minute before starting to eat.

"But, Todd," Elizabeth teased, "I have to get a head start. Otherwise, you'll finish everything in sight before I even have a chance to begin."

"Can you blame him?" Ricky Capaldo asked,

licking his fingers. "After all, it might be the best pizza in the world."

Elizabeth agreed enthusiastically. Whenever she entertained out-of-town guests, Guido's was high on her list of attractions. Most visitors, especially those from big cities, were skeptical when she told them that the little town of Sweet Valley boasted the best pizza that side of the Rockies. But one bite of a Guido's deluxe, and they were converts. Some people claimed it was the brick oven that baked up such a perfect crust. Others said it was the secret tomato-sauce recipe. Whatever the magic ingredient, no one could resist a Guido's pizza, least of all Winston Egbert, who was now on his fifth pie.

"He's doing pretty well for someone with a stomach ache, wouldn't you say?" Olivia asked.

"I'm not so sure about that," replied John. "It *is* taking him a lot longer to eat this one than the first few. And he doesn't look so hot."

"Oh, that's to be expected," Annie Whitman said. "I think he can do it." She chewed ferociously on her own slice of pizza, as if to help Winston along.

By the time Elizabeth and the others at her booth had finished their pie, talking and laughing through it, Winston, who had done nothing but eat, was starting on pie number six.

All eyes in the restaurant were on him. The foil crown had slipped off his head and now lay under the table as he gave his attention to the pizza in front of him. Winston's face was grim, and set in an expression of concentration mingled with pain. At one point he even put his head down on the edge of the table, wrapped his arms around his stomach, and began rocking back and forth, groaning softly.

"Don't give up now, Winston," Olivia called out. "You've only got another pie and a half to go."

Slowly Winston lifted his head and resumed eating. Cheers went up from the crowd, and he managed a fleeting grin for his fans and the camera.

The encouragement seemed to keep him going until he got to the last pizza. As he picked up the first slice of that last pie, Guido's was filled with cheers of excitement, wild applause, and noisy enthusiasm.

"He's going to make it!" Annie Whitman exclaimed.

But suddenly, with six-and-a-half extra-large pies down, and only a half more to go, Winston dropped the slice he was gnawing at, jumped up, and bolted toward the men's room, his face a shade of pale green.

"Oh, no . . ." Groans of disappointment went up among the crowd.

"I can't believe it," Annie said, sighing.

"So much for practice," added John Pfeifer.

The TV cameras zoomed in on the lone half pie next to the stack of empty pizza trays. "It's all over," Anna Scarpelli announced into her microphone.

"Poor Winston." Elizabeth shook her blond head. "He must feel really rotten."

A few minutes later, Winston emerged from the bathroom, a silly grin back on his lips.

"Great try," DeeDee Gordon called out over the applause that echoed off the wood-paneled walls.

"You're still the champ," someone else shouted.

"Speech, speech," Todd put in, yelling above the clamor. A few other people took up the refrain.

"If you insist," Winston said cheerfully. The room quieted down, and the cameras focused on him once more.

"First of all, even though I didn't make it, I'd like to thank you all for coming here," he began. "And if any of you want to help me out with the last pizza, it's yours for the asking." He motioned to the lukewarm remains of his seventh pie. Laughter shook the restaurant. "And I'd like to thank everyone at Guido's—especially Frank DeLuna. I hope business goes well over the next couple of months, 'cause I probably won't be coming around for a while."

"A couple of months?" Elizabeth whispered to Todd. "Is that all? Seems like he put away enough pizza today for a couple of years."

"And lastly," continued Winston, amid hoots and giggles, "I'd like to thank my mother, who sacrificed many free hours over the past couple of weeks so she could prepare practice sandwiches for me."

"Let's hear it for Mrs. Egbert," John Pfeifer called.

"And now, if you folks don't mind, I think

I'd better be getting home," Winston concluded with an impish grin. "It must be almost time for dinner!" Elizabeth burst into laughter as the Starch King began striding toward the door. *World record or no world record,* she thought, as people spilled out of the restaurant and began to go home, *you can always count on Winston for a dramatic exit.*

"Stay tuned," said KSVH's Jim Ralston, his bright smile seeming to stretch across the Wakefield's television screen. "After a word from our sponsor, Anna Scarpelli will be back to tell us about an attempt to break the world pizza-eating record—right here in Sweet Valley."

"Ooh, I can't wait." Jessica bounced up and down in the living-room armchair. "Maybe we'll get to be on the news, Liz."

"You might," Elizabeth answered her sister, "but I doubt Todd or I will, since we were sitting all the way in the back." She helped herself to a handful of Raisinettes and passed the candy dish to Betsy, who sat next to her on the sofa.

On the TV a boy of about the twins' age was working magic on a fancy new home computer. Jessica grimaced. "Please, no more computer commercials," she wailed, snatching the remote-control unit from the coffee table and switching to another channel.

"Jess!" Elizabeth said sharply. "Put that station back on. We're going to miss Winston. I thought you couldn't wait to see yourself on TV."

"I can't," Jessica said. "But I didn't want to watch that commercial. You understand, don't you?"

Elizabeth sighed. "What's the matter, Jessica? Does the sight of a computer give you a headache these days?"

Just a few weeks earlier, Jessica had gotten herself neck deep in hot water when she'd enlisted the help of the school computer genius to tamper with her math grade. As usual, Elizabeth had ended up bailing her sister out when she'd gotten caught. Afterward Jessica had succeeded in getting her math grade up on her own, but she hadn't forgotten the sticky incident. Since then, she'd gone on and on about how computers were her worst enemies.

"I don't even want to talk about it," Jessica answered dramatically. She counted to ten and switched the station back to KSVH. The boy and his computer had been replaced by a family starting the day with a new breakfast cereal.

"Whew!" Jessica exclaimed with relief. She settled down comfortably into her chair as Anna Scarpelli reappeared on the screen.

"This afternoon, a Sweet Valley youth tried to break the world pizza-eating record—and failed," announced the red-haired anchorwoman. "It happened here," she continued, as the

121

picture switched to the crowded interior of Guido's.

"Oh, wow! Can you believe it?" shrieked Jessica. "There I am."

"Where?" asked Elizabeth. "I can't find you."

"To the left of Winston, all the way by the wall." Jessica jumped off her seat and raced over to the TV. "See—there's the sleeve of my new dress," she said, pointing.

"Oh, yeah, imagine that. Your entire arm is on television," Elizabeth said unenthusiastically. "Congratulations, Jess. Can I touch you?"

"You don't have to be such a spoilsport, Liz. I know you're just jealous because you're not on." Jessica pouted as the camera focused in on Winston.

"OK, Jessica. If it'll make you happy, I admit it. I'm jealous. You looked really terrific there for a few seconds."

As Anna Scarpelli explained Winston's attempt to the TV audience, the doorbell chimed.

"I wonder who that is," Elizabeth said. "Were you expecting anyone, Jess?" Jessica shook her head. "How about you, Betsy?"

"No," answered Betsy, "but I'll go see who it is." She padded over to the entrance alcove.

Elizabeth heard the front door being pulled open. Suddenly Betsy's voice rang out. "Oh, my God!" Her shocked exclamation echoed in the living room.

Elizabeth jumped up and rushed over to the

door to see who it was. There, standing in the doorway, his eyes bloodshot, his unkempt clothes hanging loosely from his small frame, was Betsy's father, Jim Martin.

Twelve

"Steven, you're not responsible for her." Ned Wakefield's urgent tone carried out to the patio, where Jessica was working on her tan.

"But, Dad—" Steven began.

"No buts about it, son," Ned Wakefield interrupted. "Your mother and I are extremely concerned about the way you've been babying Betsy. It's not good for you. And in the long run, you're not helping her, either."

Jessica inched her deck chair closer to the open kitchen window through which the voices floated. After all, Betsy's business was Jessica's business, now that they were living under the same roof. Not that Jessica intended it to stay that way. She'd had a flash of hope the previous night, when Mr. Martin had turned up, that his daughter would go home with him. But Betsy had done no such thing. Instead, she had gone right to the phone and called Steven, to ask what she should do. Steven had responded by driving in from school immediately, to soothe Betsy's frazzled nerves and give her support.

"Dad, she needs my help," Steven was protesting, his voice now sounding loud and clear to Jessica.

"To do what?" Ned Wakefield asked. "To decide whether to go back to her father's house and try to piece together some semblance of family life? I know you mean well, Steve, but only Betsy knows if that's the right choice for her." Mr. Wakefield's voice was gentle but firm.

"Dad, please don't send her back there," Steven implored.

"Steven, no one's sending Betsy anywhere," Ned Wakefield assured his son. "Although you know as well as I do that Betsy can't live here forever."

Forever! thought Jessica. *Even one more week is one week too long. If Dad won't get rid of her now, somebody's got to.*

Ned Wakefield continued talking to his son. "Besides," he said, "you have to start concentrating on yourself a little bit more, begin putting yourself back together. And skipping a day of classes so you can take care of Betsy doesn't seem a very sensible way to go about it," he chided.

"Aw, Dad, I'm sorry," Steven mumbled. Jessica had to strain to make out his words. "But she *is* Tricia's sister."

"Steven, I feel for you. I know how devastating it must be to lose the girl you love. But making Betsy's problems your own isn't going to bring Tricia back."

"Dad, I'm the only real friend Betsy has."

"Being a friend is fine," Ned Wakefield said carefully. "We're all trying to be there for Betsy. But becoming totally responsible for another human being is an entirely different matter."

"But I—I have to take care of her," Steven said.

"Have to?" Mr. Wakefield expressed Jessica's exact thought. There was a pregnant pause. Jessica went over and sneaked a quick look through the window. Steven was sitting at the kitchen table, his head down. Ned Wakefield was bent over his son, his hand on Steven's shoulder. Suddenly Steven straightened up. Jessica ducked quickly and went back to her deck chair.

"Dad," she heard Steven say quietly, "I made Tricia a promise. Right before she died. I told her I would take care of Betsy."

So that was it! Jessica thought. It all began to make sense to her now.

"Steve, that's very generous of you," Ned Wakefield said tenderly after a few seconds. "Still, I'm sure Tricia didn't mean for you to give up your own life to spend every free moment with Betsy."

But Mr. Wakefield wasn't getting through. Steven was resolute. "Dad, I made a promise," he said. "And I intend to keep it, no matter what it takes."

126

Mr. Wakefield and Steven continued talking, but Jessica had heard enough, finally, enough to come up with a sure-fire scheme to get Betsy out of her hair—and her house—once and for all. In Steven's confession, she had found a solution to all of her problems. All she had to do was to get Betsy alone. And, if everything went according to plan, Betsy would be gone in a matter of hours.

The timing couldn't have been more perfect, Jessica reflected. Mr. and Mrs. Wakefield had gone to some friends' house after dinner for coffee and dessert. Steven was at the community center, playing a pickup game of basketball. Elizabeth was in her room writing, completely absorbed as she huddled over the typewriter. That left Betsy alone in the study with her sketch pad and charcoals.

Like a tiger ready to pounce on its prey, Jessica crept stealthily toward the partially open study door. She squeezed through it and came up behind Betsy, quietly watching her work for a few minutes. In one corner of the paper in front of her, Betsy had drawn the Wakefield kitchen table. She added a few more lines and sketched in the stove. Several more strokes, and Alice Wakefield appeared, putting on a pot of coffee.

Jessica felt her blood boil as her daily breakfast scene took shape under Betsy's hand. That was *her* kitchen, *her* family, and there was Betsy,

drawing it as if it were her own. Jessica felt like
snatching the page right out from under Betsy's
nose, to make her stop before she added one
more line. But Jessica held her anger in check.
These things had to be handled delicately.

She gave Betsy a light tap on the shoulder.
"Hi. Am I disturbing you?" she asked sweetly.

Betsy nearly jumped out of her chair. "Jessica!
You scared me!"

Good, Jessica thought to herself. *You shouldn't
start feeling like you can get too comfortable around
here.* But she assumed an appropriately apolo-
getic expression. "Oh, I'm sorry." Her voice
oozed with false sincerity. "Do you want to be
left alone?"

"Oh, no, I didn't mean it that way. I just
didn't realize anyone was here."

"I guess you were pretty caught up in your
drawing. I was too, actually. It's almost like
magic, the way you can bring things to life with
a few charcoal lines," Jessica flattered.

"Oh, it's not so amazing," Betsy said modestly.
"It's just a matter of practice. I've been doing it
practically forever."

"All I know is that I could never draw like
that."

Betsy blushed shyly. "Sure you could," she
insisted. "You're good at everything you do:
tennis, cheerleading. Why, you're one of the
most popular girls at Sweet Valley High. I'll bet
you could do almost anything you set your
mind to."

You're darned right I can, Jessica thought, *and*

128

what I want to do most is to clear some trash out of this study and out of my life! But she forced a smile. "That's sweet of you to say," she gushed. "But I haven't really done anything that impressive—not like you. I mean, look at how you've gotten yourself together after what you've been through. You've really straightened yourself out."

"Well, I can't tell you how much your family has helped," Betsy said gratefully. A faraway look came over her face. "Especially Steven," she added dreamily.

Excellent, thought Jessica. *She's playing right into my hands.* "Yeah, it's just too bad Steven can't help himself the way he's helped you," she told Betsy.

Betsy appeared puzzled. "I don't understand what you're saying."

"I'm saying that I'm worried about him," Jessica stated, taking a seat on the study sofa. "The way he's been moping around, coming home from school all the time and just sitting in his room, staring at the walls. He needs to start getting out and socializing and trying to put the past behind him. Maybe it's even time for him to think about seeing other girls."

Surprise colored Betsy's face. It was precisely the reaction Jessica wanted.

"I mean, now that you're doing OK," Jessica added.

"What does that have to do with anything?" Betsy asked, her surprise now tinged with alarm.

Jessica's carefully crafted moment of triumph

had arrived. "Well, you know. Steve promised Tricia he'd take care of you until you were back on your feet, which you are. . . ."

Betsy looked as if someone had dropped a ton of bricks on her. Her body froze in shock. Then the shock gave way to misery. "No, I didn't know," she said slowly, dropping her head in her arms.

Jessica put on a first-class show of being instantly contrite. She smacked her forehead with the palm of her hand. "Oh, my gosh, I'm s-o-o-o sorry," she wailed. "Dumb old me. How could I be so stupid?" She went over and put a comforting hand on Betsy's shoulder. "Oh, Betsy, please forgive me."

Suddenly Betsy whipped around to face Jessica, an impenetrable coldness in her eye. *"Forgive you?* Maybe I should thank you instead, for setting me straight." Her voice shook with hurt and rage. "All that attention. All that interest. It's not even for real." Betsy sprang out of her seat and began pacing the room. "Steven doesn't care about me. He's just being nice to me because of Tricia. I should have known. Why would anyone be nice to me for any other reason? No one ever has been. . . ." She stormed around the study, tears of anger and frustration streaming down her cheeks.

For a split second, Jessica almost felt sorry for her. But then Bruce Patman's smug voice echoed through her head. *"Of course no one's planning on actually having Roger and his mother move in with us. . . ."* Humiliation washed over Jessica, just thinking about Bruce's words. But that was the last insult she would take on account of Betsy Martin. Betsy was on her way out—and there was simply no room for sympathy.

"And all that encouragement about my art," Betsy continued. "All those compliments from Steven and that Jason Stone." Betsy ripped one of her sketches off the far wall of the study, crumpled it into a tight ball, and hurled it into the wastepaper basket. "And how about your dear twin? So sweet, so full of praise, but she's just playing the same game your brother is— make Betsy feel good for Tricia's sake. Right. My drawings are good enough for a professional art school. Tell me another lie." Betsy pulled down two more sketches and tore them into shreds.

"Elizabeth means well," Jessica said. "I'm sure she really does think your art is good. And so do I." Jessica knew she could afford to play the good guy now that the damage was done.

"Don't bother with the soothing words, Jessica. I don't need to be humored, not by you, or your family, or anyone else." Betsy tore down her last sketch and threw it on the floor. "I've had enough of all of you. Just leave me alone!"

"But, Betsy—" Jessica began.

"Don't 'Betsy' me. No one cares about Betsy. It's only Tricia that counts." Betsy started stuffing things into her suitcase. "I'm still not good enough for you or anyone else around here, no matter how hard I try, so why bother?"

"Well, if you're going to be like that," Jessica said, assuming her best hurt expression.

"Yes, I am. And there's nothing you can do about it," Betsy charged.

"I guess not," Jessica answered softly. "So I'll just get out of your way now," she concluded. As she turned and left the study, a triumphant smirk spread across her face. *Mission accomplished*, she congratulated herself.

Thirteen

As she entered Elizabeth's bedroom, Jessica wore her most convincing look of concern. "Oh, Liz, the most awful thing just happened," she announced sadly.

Elizabeth glanced over her shoulder. "Now what?" she questioned, a bit wearily. If she'd asked Jessica once, she'd asked her a thousand times not to interrupt her when she was working. Elizabeth sighed loudly.

"Liz, it's a real, true crisis this time," Jessica promised. "I just went in to talk to Betsy, and she was packing her bags!"

Elizabeth instantly spun around in her chair to face her twin. "What? What are you talking about?"

"Betsy's leaving. I mean—she's left already. I couldn't stop her."

"Jess. My God, what did she say?"

Jessica sat down on Elizabeth's bed. "She said she'd had enough of all of us. I don't know—I guess she just got bored with this kind of life." Jessica shook her head in imitation of despair. "What can we do? We gave her a chance to pull herself together, and she wasn't interested."

Elizabeth went over and sat down next to her sister. "I don't believe it. Where did she go? Home to her father? Without even saying good-bye?"

"Well, actually, she wasn't going home. As I was leaving the room, I heard her calling up Charlie Cashman and making plans to meet him someplace. I couldn't hear where, though."

Elizabeth groaned. "It can't be anyplace decent if she's going there with Charlie Cashman. Oh, Jessica, what on earth could have happened to send her running back to someone like him? What did we do wrong?"

Jessica avoided her sister's eyes. "I guess people like Betsy just don't change."

Elizabeth frowned. "You're so wrong, Jess. If they want to badly enough, they can. Look at Enid."

"I'd rather not," Jessica responded. "That girl can put me to sleep in about three seconds. Enid was probably more interesting the way she was before."

Elizabeth shot her sister a glare that could have frozen Niagara Falls. "Enid is terrific exactly the way she is now."

Jessica got up and walked over to Elizabeth's open window, turning her back on her twin as she gazed out to the street. Outside, a car door slammed, and she poked her head out the window for a better view. "Oh, no. It's Steven. And Jason Stone is with him!" Jessica turned back toward Elizabeth. "What are we going to tell them about Betsy?"

Elizabeth was grim. "There's only one thing we *can* tell them—the truth."

Somberly Elizabeth started down the stairs, Jessica trailing behind her. Elizabeth peered over the banister and watched her brother and Jason enter the house, laughing and talking.

Steven glanced up and caught sight of his sisters. "Liz, Jess. Hey! What's happening?" Steven's broad smile lit up his handsome face.

Elizabeth's mood sank even lower. How could she break the bad news when Steven seemed happy for the first time in weeks? She took a deep breath. "Hi, Steve, Jason. Jess and I—uh—ah—have to tell you something."

"Yeah, maybe you guys ought to sit down," Jessica added, not wanting to be left out of a dramatic moment.

"Well, we've got something to tell you, too," Steve said happily. "Don't we, Jason?"

Jason nodded. "We sure do. But why doesn't one of you go get Betsy. We want her to hear what we have to say, too. In fact," he added a little mysteriously, "the news is actually about her." There was a sparkle in his eyes.

"Our news is about Betsy, too," Elizabeth said, her solemn tone a world away from Jason's animated one.

Steven gave his sister a quizzical look, noticing for the first time the unhappiness on her face. "Liz, what is it?"

"Oh, Steve, she's gone!" Elizabeth blurted out. "Betsy's gone!"

"To her father's?" Steven asked calmly. "Yeah, she said she might go over there and talk to him. She wanted to see if they can work things out."

"No, it's not like that," Elizabeth insisted. "She left for good, suitcase and all. And she didn't go home." There was urgency in Elizabeth's words. "Jessica heard her making plans to meet Charlie Cashman somewhere."

Steven and Jason froze. "That's impossible!" Steven exclaimed.

"But it's true," Jessica put in. "Steve, I told you all along Betsy was no good."

"You're wrong, Jessica. She's changed."

"I think not," Jessica began, unfolding a carefully slanted version of the past half hour's events. "So you see," she concluded with mock despondence, "Betsy's the same as she ever was."

"I don't buy it," Steven said fiercely. "Something must have happened to make her do this."

"Well, I don't know what that something could possibly be," Jessica said innocently.

"Neither do I," Steven said, "but I intend to find out. I'm going out to look for her right now."

"I'll come with you," Jason said. "Maybe we

136

can let her know the good news before it's too late."

"Hey! What *is* the good news?" Jessica asked. "You never told us."

For a brief moment Jason looked happy again. "She got in!" he said, directing his explanation more to Elizabeth than to Jessica. "Betsy won the contest."

"She did?" Elizabeth's face lit up in excitement.

Steven's expression remained somber, though. "But art school's not going to do her any good if she's too trashed to see straight," he said grimly, bringing the conversation back to the crisis at hand. Jason's smile, too, quickly faded from his lips.

"What contest? What about art school?" Jessica pouted. "What's the big secret here?"

"Elizabeth can tell you while we're gone," Steven replied as he and Jason rushed back out into the night air.

Jason sat in the passenger seat of Steven's Volkswagen, his eyes misty behind his glasses. "I wanted to see her face when we told her," he said sadly.

"Jason, don't give up. You still might," Steven consoled his friend. "We both might." He negotiated the sharp left turn onto the road that headed toward the beach—and toward Kelly's.

"But do you think it'll make any difference now? Maybe Betsy won't even care. Maybe I'll never get a chance to prove that I meant it when I told her how good her art was."

"Look, Tricia once said that Betsy's art was the most important thing in her life, even when she was so drugged out she could barely hold a pencil. And L.A. Academy might just be the break she needs to straighten herself out for good. I think she'll care. That is, if we can find her and tell her." Steven pressed down harder on the gas pedal.

"I just hope she hasn't decided to take off, the way her father did." Jason's voice was tense.

"I know. I was thinking the same thing," Steven admitted. "But I still intend to look everywhere in Sweet Valley. If she's here, we'll locate her." He pulled into the gravel driveway of Kelly's and screeched to a halt in front of it. Both boys jumped out of the car and rushed through the open doorway into a small, smoke-filled room where loud country-and-western music spilled from the jukebox. They scanned the bar area and then poked around the back booths.

Jason shook his head, and the two friends turned to leave.

"Whatsa matter?" slurred a heavyset, red-faced man. "Not high class enough in here for the likes of you?" His tone was menacing.

"That's not it," Jason replied politely. "We're looking for a friend of ours, but she's not here."

"Oh, sure," the man snarled. But Steven and Jason had no time to argue. They raced out the door and climbed into Steven's car.

"What next?" Jason asked.

"The Shady Lady," Steven replied.

They drove in silence along the narrow road, the night time sky black except where a sliver of moon peeked out from behind the cloud cover. Each boy was lost in the fervent hope that when they got to the Shady Lady, Betsy Martin would be there.

As they pulled up in front of the bar, across from the Dairi Burger, Steven and Jason were rewarded by the sight of Charlie Cashman's Harley-Davidson.

"Betsy's got to be here," Steven said as he and Jason raced from the car.

And she was, sitting at the bar, Charlie Cashman on one side of her, Crunch McAllister on the other.

"Hey, Betsy," said Crunch. "You haven't touched your drink. What's wrong?"

Listlessly Betsy stirred her straw around in her rum and Coke. "Oh, nothing," she replied woodenly, a sad, tired expression in her large eyes. Suddenly she spotted Steven and Jason walking toward the bar. "Nothing at all," she added, quickly assuming a new, energetic tone. She took a big slug of her drink. "I'm having a great time." She began to laugh wildly and gave Crunch a wet kiss. Then she leaned toward Charlie and gave him one, too. In an instant, Betsy had become the life of the party.

Jason and Steven edged through the crowded room and came up behind Betsy.

"Betsy, are these wimps friends of yours?" Charlie asked.

Betsy spun around on her bar stool, pretending to notice Steven and Jason for the first time. "Oh, you two. I should have known." She took another swig of rum and Coke. "Well, actually, I sort of expected *you* to come bother me," Betsy said, glaring at Steven. "But you?" Now she turned her attention to Jason. "What is this? Some sort of package deal? Wherever Steven goes, you go? Why don't both of you just quit interfering in my life?" She took a drag of Crunch's cigarette and blew the smoke in Jason's face.

"Betsy," Steven said, nervously eyeing Charlie Cashman's bulky frame in his beat-up leather jacket and Crunch's black, spiked wristband, "we want to talk to you, that's all."

"Well, what if I don't want to talk to you? I was having a terrific time before you two showed up." For emphasis, she drained her glass and set it back down on the bar with a resounding thump. "Another," she said to the bartender, pointing to the empty glass. "And what are you guys drinking?" She sneered at Steven and Jason. "Shirley Temples?" Betsy laughed hysterically at her own joke. Crunch and Charlie joined in.

"On the rocks or straight up?" Charlie added.

"Good one, Charlie." Betsy roared as if it were the funniest thing in the world.

"Betsy—" Jason began timidly.

But Betsy wouldn't let him speak. "Why don't you guys give up and go home? We're busy playing games that are out of your league."

"You call drinking a game?" Steven gestured toward her refilled glass.

"Drinking—and maybe other things, too," Betsy said. There was no way she was going to allow Steven Wakefield to congratulate himself for turning her into a good little girl. "In fact" —she lowered her voice—"Charlie here just got his hands on some dynamite pot." She slung her arm around Charlie's shoulder.

But the truth was that, except for the one drink she'd downed moments earlier for the benefit of Steven and Jason, Betsy had been straight as an arrow all night. She wasn't drunk. Or high. Just hurt—very hurt. And extremely angry.

Steven drew a deep breath. "Look, Betsy—" he began.

"No, *you* look, Steven," Betsy interrupted ferociously. "I don't want you around anymore. I'm freeing you from your promise, so just beat it."

"What promise?" Steven searched Betsy's face for an answer.

"Promise? What promise?" Betsy mocked. "Don't give me that! I know all about you and your sacred promise." Betsy's rage burst out, a tornado of words that couldn't be stopped. "And there I was thinking maybe you really cared about me. Boy, you must have gotten a good laugh out of that one."

"What are you talking about?" Steven managed to ask.

141

"You know darned well what I'm talking about. I'm talking about your promise to Tricia."

Steven grew pale. "How did you find out?" he whispered.

"What difference does it make? I know. That's what counts. I know how much your wonderful kindness really means. Well, you can take your noble gestures and get lost. I never want to see your face again."

"Betsy, please listen," Steven implored.

Charlie Cashman got off his stool and took Steven by the collar. "Look, pest, the lady wants you to scram. Don't you college boys understand English?" Charlie's breath reeked of liquor.

"We're not going anywhere without Betsy," Steven told him.

Charlie released Steven from his grip and wiggled out of his jacket. He was an inch or two shorter than Steven, but much heftier. He was wearing a T-shirt with the sleeves cut off, and his arms were huge and muscular. "I'm giving you one last chance to get out of here," he snarled. "Then I'm going to mop the floor with you."

Steven stood his ground. "Charlie, this is between Betsy and me," he said.

"Oh, yeah?" Charlie swung his right fist at Steven's face. Steven was stung by the punch. He lashed out with his own fist, but it barely grazed Charlie's jaw.

"Charlie, don't!" Betsy yelled. But Charlie kept swinging. Steven took one backward step after another to get out of Charlie's reach, but he was being boxed into a corner where there would be no escape from Charlie's brutal muscle power.

"Please, stop," Betsy coaxed.

"Look, baby, I'm doing this for you," Charlie growled.

"But I want you to stop. Charlie, listen to me . . ." But it was to no avail. Steven ducked another of Charlie's punches. Suddenly Jason laid his glasses down on the bar and made a move to step in.

"Gonna help your buddy, skinny bones?" Crunch McAllister snorted. "Hey, Charlie. Better watch out for flyweight here. He's out to get you—if he can see without his glasses." Crunch guffawed loudly.

Charlie held Steven off for a moment as he took in Jason's slender build. "Hey, don't worry. If he gets in my way, I'll just blow on him. He'll go right down."

But Jason wasn't deterred by their taunts. He stepped directly in front of Charlie, shielding Steven from him.

"Outta my way, kid."

Jason didn't budge.

From her bar stool, Betsy cringed. Why was Jason being so foolish? she wondered. Charlie would flatten him in about three seconds.

"So that's the way you want it, pal." Charlie curled his upper lip at Jason. "Well, don't say I didn't warn you." He went for Jason's nose, but just before the punch connected, Jason deftly swerved his head out of the way. Charlie pitched forward, from the momentum of his empty

143

punch, and Jason swiftly hooked his left leg around Charlie's ankles. Charlie tripped and landed facedown. He got up quickly and rushed at Jason, his teeth bared. As he lashed out again, Jason grabbed Charlie's outstretched arm and flipped the large boy right over his shoulder.

All eyes in the bar were on Jason. In no time at all, Charlie Cashman was lying flat on his back, not even attempting to get up. The crowd was speechless. And the person stunned most was Betsy Martin.

Gently Jason took her by the arm. "It's time to leave," he said softly, retrieving his glasses from the bar. Betsy was too flabbergasted by Jason's performance to offer any resistance. And Crunch McAllister was too busy helping his friend up off the floor to prevent her from going. It wasn't until she, Jason, and Steven stepped into the balmy evening air that she said a word. "Jason, how did you do that?" she asked shyly.

"I'm a brown belt in karate," Jason confessed, just as shyly.

"Really?"

"Uh-huh." Jason smiled tentatively at Betsy. And for the first time she smiled back. "As a matter of fact, I'm going to try for my black belt next month."

Betsy nodded. "Judging from what you did to Charlie, I'd say it'll be a cinch for you."

"Hey, I *am* sorry about Charlie," Jason said.

"I guess he had it coming," Betsy admitted. "He shouldn't have started up. Especially since

144

I asked him not to. And besides, you were only sticking up for Steven."

"And for you," Jason added bashfully. "I didn't want to see you stuck with a creep like that all night."

"And do you think you're a better choice?" Betsy teased, not bothering to hide her admiration for Jason. After all, he had risked his safety to help her out. He owed her nothing. He had made no promises. Yet here he was, looking at her as if she were the most important person in the world. Suddenly Betsy knew that Jason had been telling the truth, that he didn't expect anything from her the way Crunch or Charlie would have. All he wanted was to be with her. She could read it in his eyes. And she was overcome by tenderness for him.

Steven watched the scene unfold, feeling a little like a third person on a bicycle built for two. But he wasn't at all unhappy at the feeling. "Listen, I'm going across to the Dairi Burger to call home and let everyone know that you're OK, Betsy," he excused himself gracefully. "Jason, why don't you tell Betsy the big news. I'll meet you both out front at the car."

Jason shot his friend a grateful smile.

"What good news, Jason?" It was the last thing Steven heard as he walked off. But he didn't have to listen to Jason's answer to know that Betsy's night was going to end more happily than she'd ever imagined.

Fourteen

The Wakefields' backyard was buzzing with activity. Enid, George, Todd, and a bunch of other kids were in the pool, engaged in a game of water tag. Alice and Ned Wakefield stood by the grill, turning hamburgers and hot dogs and watching them disappear almost as fast as they could make them. All over the lawn, people were talking and eating and enjoying the warm Saturday afternoon.

The barbecue was for Betsy, to celebrate her acceptance to art school, and though the preparations had been made at the last minute, it was a huge success. Even Jessica and Steven had finally come to a truce after a mammoth battle. For having spilled his secret, Steven had threatened to ship Jessica off to the middle of the Mojave Desert with no food or water. Jessica had retaliated by claiming that Steven had left her out of the plan to send Betsy's drawings to the L.A. Academy and had let Elizabeth in on it because he loved Elizabeth more. But now brother and sister laughed spiritedly as they tossed a Frisbee back and forth.

No one, however, was happier than Betsy. Her face glowed as she talked animatedly to Elizabeth. "You're just the greatest," she said, "submitting my pictures and having so much faith in me." The smile on her face was as bright as the afternoon sun.

"Well, entering you in the contest was mostly Jason's doing," Elizabeth said modestly. "He's a terrific guy."

"I know," Betsy responded joyfully, watching him as he joined the game of water tag. "I should have realized it right from the start. You and Steve were right about him—he's the best. And so are you and your whole family. You've all been so good to me."

Elizabeth smiled graciously.

"And you've helped me realize how important it is to have a family," Betsy continued. "I know it's just me and my father now, but I'm going to go back to him until art school starts in September and really try to make it work. Maybe I can help him the way you've helped me."

"I hope so." Elizabeth gave Betsy an impulsive hug.

"I think I'll be able to," Betsy said confidently. "Especially with friends like Jason and Steven. Which reminds me—I've got some unfinished business to attend to. Would you excuse me, Liz?"

"Sure," replied Elizabeth. She watched with curiosity as Betsy made her way over to where Steven and Jessica were tossing the Frisbee. But before she had a chance to figure out what Betsy's "unfinished business" consisted of, Elizabeth was distracted by the faint ringing of the telephone from inside the house. She hurried to answer the call.

As the Frisbee game wound down. Betsy approached Steven hesitantly. "Steve—I—um—can I talk to you for a minute?" she stammered, embarrassment coloring her delicate features. "I want to apologize."

"Apologize? For what?" Steven asked with surprise.

"Oh, you know," Betsy insisted.

Steven shook his head. "No, really, I don't."

Betsy took a deep breath. "Well, for starters, I'm sorry I came down so hard on you the other night, when you were only trying to help me."

"Oh, don't worry about it," Steven said lightly.

"No, I'm not finished," Betsy told him. "I'm also sorry I took all your attention the wrong way." Betsy's face was crimson with embarrassment, but she pressed on. "I know you were having a hard enough time, even without me—um—hanging around all the time." She lowered her head.

Oh, please, thought Jessica, surveying her brother and Betsy from a few yards away. *Spare me the corny-apology scene*. But Betsy and Steven were oblivious to Jessica's scrutinizing stare.

"Betsy . . ." Gently Steven tilted her chin up so her gaze met his. "I really did want to make things easier for you," he said in a soft voice.

Betsy nodded. "I realize that now, and I can see why you made that promise to Tricia. I just wish I had understood sooner how you were feeling. I'm sorry for all the trouble I caused you."

"Betsy, there's no need for apologies. It's been a rough time for both of us." A sad expression spread across Steven's handsome face. "Tricia was a very special human being."

Betsy nodded silently, her eyes shining with unshed tears. Impulsively, Steven reached over and hugged her.

"Hey—what's going on here?" Jason's voice boomed out good-naturedly. He dried himself off with a towel as he walked over to where Betsy and Steven were standing.

Steven flashed a warm grin at his friend. Betsy reached out and pulled Jason over to them, including him in an affectionate, three-way bear hug.

Oh, brother, thought Jessica, standing up and stretching her slender body. *This is getting too cozy for words*. She turned on her heel and walked off, leaving her brother, Jason, and Betsy behind her. She cast a look around the lush lawn to see what Elizabeth was up to and caught sight of her coming out of the house. On her face was a dazed expression. Jessica rushed over to her twin's side. "Liz, what's wrong? You look like you just saw a ghost."

"It's even stranger than that," Elizabeth said slowly. "Olivia Davidson just called. Roger's mother died this morning."

"Gee, that's too bad." Jessica shook her head. "But it's not that surprising."

"That wasn't all Liv told me," Elizabeth continued. "Jessica, you're not going to believe this."

"Try me," Jessica said impatiently.

"Well, do you know who Paul Patman was?"

"Sure. Bruce Patman's uncle. The one who was killed in a plane crash. He was even more loaded than Bruce's dad. But what's that got to do with Roger Barrett?"

"Jess, it turns out Mr. Barrett wasn't Roger's real father. Even Roger didn't know the truth. But now it's out. His real father was Paul Patman!"

Jessica's jaw dropped open in astonishment. "You mean—?" She groped for words.

Elizabeth nodded. "Yes, Jess. Roger is going to live with the Patmans. What's more, he's just become the richest boy in Sweet Valley!"

Now Roger is as rich as Bruce, but how much will he have to change to fit in to the Patmans' world? Find out in Sweet Valley High #16, RAGS TO RICHES.

SWEET VALLEY HIGH

☐	26741	DOUBLE LOVE #1	$2.75
☐	26621	SECRETS #2	$2.75
☐	26627	PLAYING WITH FIRE #3	$2.75
☐	26746	POWER PLAY #4	$2.75
☐	26742	ALL NIGHT LONG #5	$2.75
☐	26813	DANGEROUS LOVE #6	$2.75
☐	26622	DEAR SISTER #7	$2.75
☐	26744	HEARTBREAKER #8	$2.75
☐	26626	RACING HEARTS #9	$2.75
☐	26620	WRONG KIND OF GIRL #10	$2.75
☐	26824	TOO GOOD TO BE TRUE #11	$2.75
☐	26688	WHEN LOVE DIES #12	$2.75
☐	26619	KIDNAPPED #13	$2.75
☐	26764	DECEPTIONS #14	$2.75
☐	26765	PROMISES #15	$2.75
☐	26740	RAGS TO RICHES #16	$2.75
☐	24723	LOVE LETTERS #17	$2.50
☐	26687	HEAD OVER HEELS #18	$2.75
☐	26823	SHOWDOWN #19	$2.75
☐	24947	CRASH LANDING! #20	$2.50

<u>Prices and availability subject to change without notice.</u>

Buy them at your local bookstore or use this convenient coupon for ordering:

Bantam Books, Inc., Dept. SVH, 414 East Golf Road, Des Plaines, Ill. 60016

Please send me the books I have checked above. I am enclosing $_____ (please add $1.50 to cover postage and handling). Send check or money order —no cash or C.O.D.'s please.

Mr/Mrs/Miss _____

Address _____

City _____ State/Zip _____

SVH—4/87

Please allow four to six weeks for delivery. This offer expires 10/87.

Bantam Books presents a Super

Surprise

Three Great Sweet Dreams Special Editions

Get to know characters who are just like you and your friends . . . share the fun and excitement, the heartache and love that make their lives special.

☐ 25884 MY SECRET LOVE #1 by
Janet Quin-Harkin. $2.95

☐ 26168 A CHANGE OF HEART #2 by
Susan Blake. $2.95

☐ 26292 SEARCHING FOR LOVE $2.95

EXCITING NEWS FOR ROMANCE READERS

Love Letters—the all new, hot-off-the-press Romance Newsletter. Now you can be the first to know:

What's Coming Up:
* Exciting offers
* New romance series on the way

What's Going Down:
* The latest gossip about the SWEET VALLEY HIGH gang
* Who's in love . . . and who's not

Who's Who:
* The real life stories about SWEET DREAMS cover girls
* The true facts about SWEET DREAMS authors

Who's New:
* Meet Kelly Blake
* Find out who's a *Winner* And much, much more!

Fill out this coupon, mail it in, and this spring your free copy of *Love Letters* is on its way to you. *Love Letters*—you're going to love it.

BANTAM
SHOP-AT-HOME
C·A·T·A·L·O·G

Special Offer
Buy a Bantam Book
for only 50¢.

Now you can order the exciting books you've been wanting to read straight from Bantam's latest listing of hundreds of titles. *And* this special offer gives you the opportunity to purchase a Bantam book for only 50¢. Here's how:

By ordering any five books at the regular price per order, you can also choose any other single book listed (up to $4.95 value) for only 50¢. Some restrictions do apply, so for further details send for Bantam's listing of titles today.

Just send us your name and address and we'll send you Bantam Book's SHOP AT HOME CATALOG!

BANTAM BOOKS, INC.
P.O. Box 1006, South Holland, ILL. 60473

Mr./Mrs./Miss/Ms. _____
(please print)

Address _____

City_____ State _____ Zip _____
FC(B)—11/85

Printed in the U.S.A.